MAN
CRAZY

MAN CRAZY

JOYCE CAROL OATES

A NOVEL

A WILLIAM ABRAHAMS BOOK

DUTTON

ACKNOWLEDGMENTS

Parts of this novel have appeared, in different forms, in:

"Ghost Girls" in *American Short Fiction*, 1995; and in *The Best American Short Stories 1996*.

"Marsena Sportsman's Club" in *TriQuarterly*, 1995.

"See You in Your Dreams" in *Southern Review*, 1995.

"Easy Lay" in *Ploughshares*, 1996.

"Lost Kittens" in *TriQuarterly*, 1997.

"Man Crazy" in *Blind Spot*, 1997.

DUTTON
Published by the Penguin Group
Penguin Putnam Inc., 375 Hudson Street,
New York, New York 10014, U.S.A.
Penguin Books Ltd, 27 Wrights Lane,
London W8 5TZ, England
Penguin Books Australia Ltd, Ringwood,
Victoria, Australia
Penguin Books Canada Ltd, 10 Alcorn Avenue,
Toronto, Ontario, Canada M4V 3B2
Penguin Books (N.Z.) Ltd, 182–190 Wairau Road,
Auckland 10, New Zealand

Penguin Books Ltd, Registered Offices:
Harmondsworth, Middlesex, England

First published by Dutton, an imprint of Dutton Signet, a member of Penguin Putnam Inc.

First Printing, September, 1997
10 9 8 7 6 5 4 3 2

 REGISTERED TRADEMARK—MARCA REGISTRADA

LIBRARY OF CONGRESS CATALOGING-IN-PUBLICATION DATA:
Oates, Joyce Carol, 1938–
    Man crazy : a novel / Joyce Carol Oates.
      p. cm.
    "A William Abrahams book."
    ISBN 0-525-94232-7 (acid-free paper)
    I. Title.
  PS3565.A8M35   1997
  813'.54—dc21
                                  97-12725
                                      CIP

Printed in the United States of America
Set in Garamond Book
Designed by Leonard Telesca

PUBLISHER'S NOTE

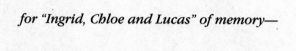

for "Ingrid, Chloe and Lucas" of memory—

PROLOGUE:

Tell Me of Your Life

I'd been brought to the hospital in wrist shackles. In a van marked CHAU CO WOMEN'S DET CT. In a shapeless gray smock, bare legs and laceless sneakers. They'd taken away the laces because I was on suicide watch at the detention center but I would never hang myself with *shoelaces!*—that's got to be a joke. I would never hang myself in any way, it's an ugly death. I've been close to strangled and I know.

Also: the shock of somebody finding the hanging body is too great. You can't inflict that kind of ugliness on an innocent bystander.

O.K.: maybe I did try to poke myself with a fork smuggled back to my cell after supper one night. My head was hurting and word was, I could almost hear the whispering, my life was over anyway. *Dog-girl! Dog-girl! Dog-girl!* but when I'd look around, all their eyes were turned away. There's a guard, happened to be a black woman, stands by the door of the dining hall overseeing a big plastic bucket and you drop your used fork and spoon inside, no knives of course, and this guard has got to be alert and cagey but it's a boring post and naturally her thoughts wander. I'd slip into her head through her glazy eyes and saw the shuffling lines of us, gray smocks, battered faces and scared eyes, a leakage of pity and disgust and a numbness so I knew the guard wasn't alert to me, a tall downlooking sallow-faced white girl and I carried out the fork in a crease of my skirt.

Just to get a vein going, that was the only purpose. To see *Am I real? Any of this?*

I was not on methadone, I was not a junkie. But you feel the need, the need builds up, every forty-eight hours or so. It's a fact, it's human anatomy. Neurology. We all want to explode. If you can't come one way, you come some other way. I pick at my skin, too. My face. Don't tell me it's a beautiful face and I'm scarring it, I've heard that before. Or my eyes, et cetera. All I know is there's this tightness in my skin like it's a drum's skin stretched to bursting, and a pounding heat in it like fever. You people staring at me in pity, disgust, superiority whispering *Dog-girl!*

Always had this bad habit since I was a little girl, Momma despaired of me. Maybe because Momma used to be so beautiful, I needed to hurt one of us? Picking at my face till it bleeds. These rashes that flare up out of nowhere, pimples hard as grit, insect bites— my sharp fingernails find their own way, greedy for what they find. Asleep, or awake. Dig till a little blood starts!

Then I feel better. Almost better.

As for the fork they confiscated. One of those cheap dime-store tin things, prongs dull as the handle. Stabbed myself in the shower in fury and mockery that the fork was so fucking inadequate, you know?—like it was a joke, against me. *Look how despised Dog-girl is, a fork so dull is all Satan has allotted her.*

* * *

An owl-looking matron from the detention center and a sheriff's deputy, male, sexy in that sag-eyed way turns some women on, took me to the hospital. Following the yellow arrows to PSYCHIATRIC SERVICES. I figured I would be given shock treatments as punishment and maybe that would cleanse me.

My long straggly curly blond hair gone thin on the sides from starvation and my picked-at face and the bandage on my left arm and—for sure!—the wrist shackles drew a lot of attention in the hospital. Like on TV. You'd see a hospital worker or a visitor or a patient in a wheelchair or even ambulatory pushing an IV on a gurney watching us approach, the three of us abreast, their eyes widening with interest as we passed and they'd freeze and turn to watch us till we were down the corridor and out of sight. *Is that the one—? That girl—? The one who—?* Inside my hot eyelids comes a quick dream of seeing myself through a stranger's eyes. Wondering what judgment to pass on this person who's *me*.

There was a doctor, I didn't see his face. I was crying, and I was ashamed, O.K. I did want to die, that was my secret. And him saying in that slow kind pushy voice like something prying a shell open *Tell me of your life, Ingrid. We want to make you well.*

Saying, *I'm a doctor, I don't judge.*

And I could not speak. Nor lower my hands from my face. My face that is scarred if you look in such bright light. This man saying, repeating *You've suffered a severe trauma but now you're safe, and you're going to be all right. Will you trust me?*

I shook my head I don't know.
Why won't you look at me, Ingrid?
I shook my head I don't know.
No? Will you speak to me, then?
No?

Ghost Girls

This story I want to tell began in upstate New York, in the Chautauqua Mountains, in August 1972.

It was a time when Momma had to take us—her and me—into hiding. The first time I saw what isn't there to be seen.

Arrangements had been made for Daddy's friend Vaughn Brownlee he'd known in Vietnam to fly us from Marsena where we'd been living to Wolf's Head Lake in the Chautauqua Mountains where we'd stay at somebody's camp. How long? Momma wanted to know, and Brownlee shrugged saying, As long as required.

I was five years old and sharp for my age, Smartass they called me but I didn't know if Momma and me had to go into hiding because Daddy had enemies who wanted to hurt us or if it was Daddy himself who was the danger.

Some things you know without asking. Other things, you can't ask. And you never know.

That airstrip at Marsena!—just a single unpainted hangar outside town, rusty corrugated tin roof and rotted wind sock slapping listless in the breeze, a single dirt runway between cornfields you'd swear wouldn't be long enough for even the smallest plane to rise from.

On the far side of one of the cornfields, out of sight from the airport, was the Chautauqua River, narrow as a creek above Marsena, rocky white-water rapids. There were airports Daddy used in those years at Mt. Ephraim, Tintern Falls, South Lebanon and each one of them is clear in my memory but Marsena is the most vivid because of what happened afterward. Also, the biggest plane you could rent at Marsena was an ex–Air Force trainer with a canopied open cockpit, a two-seater that flew at an altitude of twelve thousand feet, higher than any of the other planes, that was Daddy's favorite. It was a Vultee basic trainer—VULTEE in fading black letters on the fuselage—Daddy said of another era, World War II, not his war but his own father's now gone. That past spring he'd taken Momma up in the Vultee and they flew to Lake Ontario and back, gone for almost an hour and I kept having to go to the bathroom to pee in the concrete-stinking stall where the hard dry shells of beetles lay underfoot, at last returning to the airport and buzzing the hangar so Gus Speer the owner ran out shaking his fist, and the others hanging around watching and drinking beer on a Sunday afternoon and Daddy in the Vultee was circling the field, landing in a deafening blurred roar like a dream you can't wake from, Fucking-O perfect landing they said. And taxiing back to the hangar, and the sun glaring like knife blades off the wings. And the terrible wind of the twin propellers dying. And Momma emerged from the cockpit shaken and white-faced and not so pretty, dazed pulling off her helmet and goggles and trying to smile squinting at me and the others, and climbing down half-falling into Daddy's arms, groping as if she couldn't see him clearly, nor the ground which must have seemed strange to her, so solid, but still Momma was smiling, her happy smile, her mouth bright red like something shiny pressed into soft white bread dough. And there was the promise Daddy would take me up in the Vultee some Sunday afternoon, too.

One of these days, Birdie, Daddy would say. Smiling the way he did. Like there was some secret understanding between him and me, even Momma couldn't guess.

Birdie wasn't my name!—my name is Ingrid.

Momma pulled me by the hand murmuring under her breath Oh God, oh Jesus, and there was Brownlee waiting for us on the other side of the hangar, with a look of a man who isn't happy with waiting. His big sunburnt face like a red cabbage, and his mouth working—he was always chewing something, a big wad of gum, or a plug of tobacco. Brownlee was heavier than Daddy in those days, in his flying clothes a sky blue nylon zip-up jacket and oil-spotted khakis, brown helmet and goggles that made him look like a big beetle on its hind legs. Brownlee waved at us and Momma pulled me along. The plane he'd be flying was one of the small ones, a two-seater Cessna silvery yellow across the wings, with fading black trim. One propeller. Seeing it, hearing the motor, I pulled back on Momma's arm and she didn't like that. She was half-carrying half-pushing me. "Honey, stop crying!" she said. "Crying never did anybody any Goddamned good."

I didn't know I'd been crying. Momma's eyes were wet, too. Shining like tarnished-coppery pennies.

I knew not to cross Momma in certain of her moods. However scared I was. Just let myself go limp, a rag doll, boneless.

Brownlee stared at Momma like it hurt him to see

her, the way men stared at Momma in those days. Saying, "O.K., Chloe, let's go. We need to land up there before dark."

Brownlee and Daddy had been Navy pilots in the War, Airman First Class they called each other, saluting, sneering like kids. Like the words tasted bad in their mouths. But the War was over for them now. That's some of the trouble, Momma said.

Brownlee helped Momma into the Cessna stooping beneath the wing, then I climbed inside onto her lap. It was unlawful for Brownlee to take us like this, no belt for me, the space cramped smaller than a motor-cycle sidecar. But Gus Speer who owned the airport was a friend of Daddy's and Brownlee's and no friend of the law.

Brownlee shut Momma's door. She latched it from the inside. We watched as Brownlee spat into the dirt and hitched up his khaki trousers slung low on his hips and went to start the propeller, that way of squinting that was Daddy's way, too, starting a pro-peller by hand. Slow at first like a ceiling fan you can follow the turning of the blade with your eyes then faster and faster until you can't make out the blade any longer only the blurred circular motion it would hurt you to set your hand inside.

"Now sit still, Ingrid," Momma said. "And be brave, O.K.?"

Brownlee spat out the rest of what was in his mouth and climbed into the cockpit behind us with a grunt. The plane creaked beneath his weight. Momma was holding me tight murmuring under her breath Oh God, oh Jesus, her quick warm breath, her beery-sour breath in my face. She'd been drinking beer in the car, her and

the man who'd driven us to the airport whose name I
didn't know, a six-pack she'd taken from the refrigerator
on our way out the door. No time for Momma to throw
together more than a few things of ours in her zebra-
stripe tote bag. We'd only been living in the farmhouse
off a dirt road outside Marsena for about two weeks,
there were other people living there too and trouble of
some kind and Daddy drove away in the night and next
day men came by to ask about him, yesterday morning
two Eden County sheriff's deputies. The first thing you
hear when a police car turns up the drive is radio voices,
ratchety and loud. Looking for Lucas Boone, they said.
The German shepherd was barking like crazy straining
at his leash, neck hairs bristling and ears laid back and
one of the deputies had his pistol drawn ready to fire
but Happy was tied to a clothesline post and Momma
was screaming, Don't shoot him please!—he's no harm
to you! and the deputy didn't shoot Happy.

Brownlee was asking Momma was she belted in?
O.K.?

Momma said, "O.K." Hugging me tight.

Brownlee started the Cessna in motion, taxiing out
the runway. Slow at first. The wheels bumping. Gus
Speer in his overalls lifted a hand as we passed, a worried look on his face. We passed the row of parked
planes, the Vultee at the end. The sun was beginning to
set like fire melting into the sky atop the cliff above the
river. Momma whispered to me gripping me tight saying
it was a short flight, we'd be there before we knew it,
just stay still. I understood that if there was any danger
Momma would be holding me like that, Momma would
never give me up. Daddy had said these little shithead
civilian planes were the dangerous ones not the bomber

jets he'd flown in Nam but I was thinking even if we crashed and died I would be safe in Momma's arms.

The plane was rushing along the runway and the wheels began to skip. With Brownlee behind us it was like no one was the pilot, no one in control just Momma and me staring past the plane's nose and the spinning blades. There was a sickening lurch into the air, straight into the wind. The hard-packed dirt rushing beneath like a torrent. Weeds coated with dust, and a stack of scrap lumber and corrugated tin in a field, and beyond the cornstalks in almost-uniform rows dun-colored and bleached in the heat of August looking like paper cutouts. We were in the air now, and banking right. Headed north where the sky was dense with clouds. We saw telephone poles and wires above the highway, and the asphalt highway too, and a lone pickup truck moving on it, everything falling suddenly away as if sucked down. And now the Chautauqua River was visible, the color of tin, rippling red streaks from the sunset, a long snaky stretch of it out of sight. The plane was shuddering so in the wind, the engine was so loud, you would think it would break into pieces, it would never hold.

"Here we go," Momma said, raising her voice so I could hear her over the propeller, "—we're having *fun*, aren't we?"

She knows I love her, I'm crazy about her, doesn't she? It's just a hard time right now.

Of course she knows, Luke.

And you, too?

Momma's voice dipped so I almost couldn't hear lying still not breathing my eyes shut tight so I was seeing flashes of light like fireflies against my eyelids. *That's what I've been saying, darling. Me, too.*

Because I wouldn't want any further misunder-standing. Not at this crucial time.

Luke, no! There's no misunderstanding on my part.

That's how people get hurt. They cause their own sorrow. If things get confused.

That can't happen with us, we've been together too long. You know that.

I know it, and I want you to know it, too. And her.

Ingrid's too young to understand, darling.

Well, you explain to her, then. You're her mother for Christ's sake.

North of Marsena, in the mountains, everything was changed. The wind was stronger and Brownlee seemed to be having trouble keeping on course. I'd been asleep on Momma's lap, the wind was so loud shaking the plane, voices shouting past, I couldn't stay awake. My drooling mouth against Momma's soft breast so finally it hurt her and she woke me up.

Outside the sky was darkening in the direction we were headed. Clouds roiling up at the horizon thick with storms, heat lightning flashing in the distance like eyes blinking. Below were thick expanses of woods, foothills and mountains and curving streams and pockets of low-lying clouds. The sun was just a narrow funnel of rapidly diminishing pale red light and it scared and excited me seeing it from such a height like we were above the sun, we could see it sinking over. *The edge of the world that's always there whether you see it or not or know of it or not. So close you could be sucked over easy as sleep.*

Momma pointed out Wolf's Head Lake, or what she thought was the lake, below us. The valley was a deep ditch of shadow smudged with mist. A mirrorlike patch of water inside. We were starting to descend, not smoothly but in lurches, like going down steps in the dark. I wasn't afraid, with Momma holding me so tight. I stared at the light skimming the mountaintops, the pines beginning to become distinct, individual. And there was a road!—curving alongside one of the mountains, suddenly visible. And another road, crossing a strip of water. Narrow lakes like fingers, so many of them, and closer in farmland and pastures in neat rectangles, I could see cattle grazing, the tin-glaring roof of a barn, a truck moving along a highway. We were coming in to land—where? A narrow airstrip ahead. The plane's shadow wasn't visible skimming the ground below, the sun was too far gone.

Momma said worried in my ear, "Hold on, darling. It might be a little—" but already the runway was coming up fast, our little plane swerved in a gust of wind and Brownlee cursed behind us and there was a split second when he might've raised the nose and risen again to circle for another try but instead he brought us down clumsily hitting the ground so Momma and I screamed and the plane went bouncing and skipping and finally rolled dazed along the runway the right wing tilted almost skimming the ground. We came to a skidding stop at the end of the runway, a field beyond, as the first fat hissing raindrops began to fall.

Momma was half-sobbing screaming at Brownlee, "You asshole! All of you! You want to kill us don't you!"

*   *   *

A woman friend of Brownlee's named Maude was waiting for us at the airport and by the time we drove out to Wolf's Head Lake to the hunting camp it was dark and raining hard. The mountain road curved, the car's yellow headlights flew ahead. Where we'd all be staying wasn't a house exactly, they called it a lodge, single-story with missing shingles and a crumbling stone chimney and a rotted porch across the width of the front. Wild bushes pushing up close. Scrap lumber, an old auto chassis in the yard. Inside it smelled of kerosene. There were few pieces of furniture—a battered sofa, some chairs—and no carpet on the loose-fitting floorboards. Above the fireplace stuffed with debris was a deer's handsome mounted head and antlers. From Daddy I knew to count the points: there were ten. I stood staring at the deer on the wall seeing his fur was faded to the color of sand and mangy with time, his dark-glassy eyes were coated with dust.

Brownlee said, like he was playing Daddy, in that way Daddy would with me, "He can't see you, Birdie: he's blind."

I said, "I know that."

Brownlee said, smiling, and winking at Momma and the woman named Maude, "I mean he's blinder than blind, poor fucker. His eyes are glass."

Momma said, "Did you shoot him, Vaughn?—he's your trophy?"

"Hell, no. I'm not a hunter. I don't give a shit about hunting animals."

Brownlee said this and there was a silence and the woman named Maude laughed like she was clearing her throat, and Momma said nothing just took my hand and pulled me along into one of the back rooms where we'd be sleeping. When she switched on the light the first thing we saw was something dead on the floor beneath a window—"Jesus!" Momma said. She thought it was a bat, kept me from getting too close. I stared seeing two long columns of black ants leading to it from the wall.

Not Death only but what follows, you don't want to know.

The things I saw, in Nam, Daddy said, *oh sweet fucking Christ you don't want to know.*

Momma was breathing hard. Ran her hands through her hair in that way of hers, angry, but like she's about to cry, too. Instead lighting a cigarette from out of her tote bag. She laughed, her eyes shining so you'd swear she was happy. "What the hell, honey, right? We're alive, and we're here."

"Is Daddy going to be with us?"

Momma was stamping the ants to death. Both feet. These tinsel-looking flat sandals, and her feet delicate, narrow, bluish-pale, red polish on the toenails chipped. Momma was wearing her white rayon slacks fitted close to her body, her shiny white plastic belt that made her waist so tiny, red jersey top that pulled across her breasts. A thin gold chain with a green cross on it Daddy said was jade, bought in Saigon. Momma was so young, only twenty-three. She was just a girl, wasn't she. And so beautiful, it hurt you to look but you had to look. Silky white-blond hair, her brown eyes set deep, her mouth that seemed always pouting, even when she smiled. Momma was smoking her cigarette at the same time pushing the dead thing away with her foot, toward the door, the door was open and in the front room Brownlee and the woman named Maude were talking. Sometimes when Momma spoke up her voice was so loud and laughing-angry you'd be surprised, and it was like that now.

"Say, Vaughn—Airman First Class Brownlee—get your ass in here, will you? There's something nasty scaring my little girl I want taken care of *now*."

I was disappointed, Wolf's Head Lake wasn't close by the damn old "lodge" at all. A mile away, at least, down a bumpy dirt lane. You couldn't hear any waves, and you couldn't smell any water. Outside everywhere you looked, no moon, no stars and nothing but pitch-black night.

Maude had brought some food in grocery bags that ripped and spilled on the counter and she and Momma made supper finally though it took a long while, always it seemed to take a long while to make meals in those days because people got interrupted, there was drinking to be done, cigarettes lit and relit, pots and pans missing or nonexistent and often there was a problem locating cutlery—what was called "silverware." And there were arguments, discussions. But finally a meal would be prepared like this late-night supper which was hamburger patties grilled in the fireplace, big doughy-soft buns the size of a man's hand, and ketchup, and relish sugary-tasting as candy, and Frito-Lay potato chips the kind that came in the cardboard box and smelled of the cardboard—we were all starving, especially Brownlee who as he ate blinked like his eyes were welling tears. And there was beer for them, just water for me that Momma wasn't too happy about—rust-streaked trickling out of the kitchen faucet.

It started then, my way of eating. If it's ground meat like hamburger pink or runny-red in the center I'll eat just the edges shutting my eyes, if it's muscle-meat like steak or cutlets where you can see the texture of the flesh I can't eat it at all unless I'm drunk or stoned and somebody can talk me out of seeing what it is.

It was around midnight when we were eating and headlights flashed up the drive and I ran to see if it was Daddy but it wasn't—two men I'd never seen before, one of them with spidery tattoos up and down his arms. They'd brought more six-packs of beer, and a bottle of Four Roses, and a little plastic Baggie of what Momma called "dope"—which she said scared her for the weird thoughts it made her think but she couldn't say no to trying it most of the time. Later on they played cards, Momma and Maude and Brownlee who got happy and loud when he drank and the man with the tattooed arms whose name was Skaggs and the other man, a little younger, with a mustache, moist yellowish-dark eyes like Happy's eyes, whose name was McCarry. McCarry's hair was greased back in quills and his skin was pimply but he was sweet-boy-looking sitting close beside Momma offering to help her with her cards but Momma laughed saying no thanks, friend, she didn't need anybody's help she'd been playing gin rummy since the age of ten.

"And winning my fair share, too."

"*That*, Miz Boone, I don't doubt."

It was one of those times that any minute Daddy would drive up and come through the door except he didn't and I started to cry and Momma said I was tired and it's time for bed and I said no I didn't want to go to bed not in that nasty bed I was scared I said and every-

body was looking at me holding their cards, Momma's
voice was soft and pleading and guilty-sounding and
she was stroking my face she said was feverish, my skin
was sunburnt, my hair all tangles and I kicked at her
and she grabbed my ankles to stop me and a little table
fell over with some empty beer cans on it and a styrofoam cup used as an ashtray and Maude helped Momma
and I squirmed away from them but Momma caught me
harder, carried me into our room, I went limp and
boneless and too tired to cry or protest, Momma shined
a flashlight into the corners of the room and under the
bed to see there wasn't anything waiting to hurt me,
Momma pulled off my T-shirt and slacks and laid me
atop the lumpy bed that creaked and pulled a spread
over me, it was a thin chenille spread with a smell
of damp and mildew, a familiar smell like the smell of
Black Flag insecticide that was an undercurrent in the
air, you could never escape. Momma said, "Things are
going to be O.K., Ingrid," kissing me on the cheek, her
kiss tasting of beer and cigarette smoke, "—we'll make it
up to you, honey, we promise." I grabbed her hair to
pull her down next to me but she slapped my hand
away and then she was gone back out to the card game
and I'd wake up hearing low murmurous voices like
water rushing past, the noise of the water churning
white and frothy below the dam at Marsena, Daddy lifting me on his shoulder to see it better, except Daddy
wasn't here, I was somewhere hearing men's voices
I didn't know, now and then they'd laugh loud, and
women's voices too, that rising-wailing sound of wom-
en's voices late at night. *Oh you bastard! You Goddamned motherfucker-bastard!*—a woman's voice loud
in teasing.

Waking then when Momma came tiptoeing into the room carrying her sandals. Trying to be quiet but colliding with a chair and cursing under her breath and climbing onto the bed and the springs creaking beneath her and she was too exhausted even to draw the cover partway over her, just fell asleep. A wet gurgling click in her throat. "Momma," I whispered. "Momma, I hate you." She didn't hear, she was starting to snore, not like Daddy snored but softer and discontinuous like asking questions? each little breathy snore a question? and I smelled Momma's special smell when she was tired and hadn't washed in a while, I tried to nudge into her arms so she might hold me like she used to all the time when I was little, "Momma, I love you," I said. Big Mommy Cat she'd called herself and I was Baby Kitten and we'd nap together during the day sometimes, sometimes in the backseat of the car if Daddy was late getting back but Momma was deep asleep now and didn't give a damn about me. I was wide awake. Those shrill insect noises outside in the night like tiny chain saws and there were Goddamned mosquitoes in the room that'd come through the broken screen drawn by the smell of our blood. Bites on my face that swelled and itched, I scratched at them hard and mean to spite Momma, it was Momma's fault I was so bit up, in the morning she'd be sorry.

Now this happened. I'd been hearing these voices thinking it was Maude and somebody else, but after a while I decided it was not, it was girls' voices, *little girls somewhere outside*. I climbed down from the bed where Momma was sleeping so hard and I went to the window to look out and the sky surprised me, it was lighter than the trees, a hard-glaring blue like ink.

The insects were singing like crazy but over on top of them were these girls' voices, —*eena?* one of them was saying, —*eena?* like it was part of a name. I couldn't make out any words, I pressed my face against the dirty screen and at first I couldn't see anybody but then I saw them, I'd been looking at them not recognizing what it was, these figures toward the front of the lodge by the porch. The girls were a little older than me I estimated, and they were sisters. I knew that. They were sisters crouched and hiding, the taller one hugging the other who was crying trying to make her hush, —*eena?* —*eena?* I wondered if they'd just crawled out from under the porch? or were they about to crawl under the porch? Was somebody after them, was that why they were so scared? Out there in the dark, in the dripping bushes. If they were Maude's children where'd they been earlier, why hadn't they eaten with us, I wanted to wake Momma to ask but didn't dare, I knew that kind of hard panting sleep of Momma's, skin clammy with sweat.

The girls made me feel sad. And scared something was going to happen that couldn't be stopped.

How long I listened to them not hearing any actual words but only their voices, I don't know. Pressing my face against the screen until finally the voices went away, the little girls were gone without my noticing and there was just the night insects like before, crazy and loud. And Momma's breathless little pants and snores in the bed behind me.

"Momma?—hey!"

It was early morning. I tried to wake Momma but she groaned and shoved me away. She was still sleeping hard, her mouth open, eyelids fluttering and twitching like she was arguing with somebody in a dream. I laughed seeing Momma's face swollen with mosquito bites, her upper lip was swollen twice its normal size. Her red jersey top was pulled off one shoulder and her bra strap, which was white, but a kind of yellow-white, was twisted. Momma'd kicked the chenille cover onto the floor, I saw her white rayon slacks were stained, she wasn't going to like that. I touched her in stealth like I'd do sometimes when she didn't know, when she was flat on her back asleep I'd touch her stomach, that's where I'd come from Momma had told me, I'd stare and stare wondering was it so, how could I be so little, wouldn't I suffocate, it scared me to think of it and so I did not think of it except at such times and even then I didn't think of it, I said, "Momma damn you!"—gave up trying to wake her and went into the front room barefoot quiet as I could hoping nobody would see me, I hoped Skaggs and McCarry were gone, the room was empty except for the buck's head above the mantel, those glassy-dusty eyes watching me.

Always, there's been somebody watching me. Holding me in His vision, so I can't escape even if I wished to escape.

This was a room like so many rooms where there'd been a party and the smells of such a room in the morning, the stale smoke, the beer spillage, potato chips—these were smells I knew. Scattered over the table they'd been using which was a wooden table with scars and burns in it were beer cans and bottles and styrofoam cups and ashes and butts, a flattened Frito-Lay box, playing cards. I always liked playing cards, watching Daddy and Momma and their friends at their games, the cards were precious things because adults handled them with such importance, you didn't ever interrupt them at a serious moment, especially you didn't interrupt any man. There was the queen of hearts on the floor I picked up to look at, also the ace of clubs, the cards were sticky and the reverse side disappointing—no picture just a design of black and mustard-yellow stripes.

Outside in the puddled-dirt drive Maude's car was the only car, Skaggs and McCarry were gone. There'd been times when people who showed up late at night were not gone in the morning nor would be gone for days, a friend of Daddy's once only a few months ago before Marsena in a back bedroom shouting and crying and Daddy had to watch over him, try to talk to him Momma said, he'd had a shotgun with him and some grievance to make right and Daddy and Brownlee had finally talked him out of it but it was a long time before he went away.

I went outside. Barefoot onto the splintery porch. Some of the planks too were rotted, you had to be careful where you walked.

I was shivering looking to where the little girls had been hiding—but I couldn't see anything. Tall grasses gone to seed, a straggly bush speckled with aphids. Momma wouldn't like me going barefoot out here, but I crawled under the railing and jumped down to the ground and it was strange how still my mind got, and how empty like I was waiting for something to fill it. "Hey? Are you here? Where are you?—I saw you," I said, like calling out but not raising my voice much, too scared to raise my voice. I squatted down to look under the porch but couldn't see much—it was a nasty dark cobwebby place, smelling of damp. That was when I started shivering hard and jumped up and backed away.

Walked around the yard, in the high grass that was wet from the night, and some of it sharp against my feet, and cold. My eyes swung up seeing how clear the sky was this morning, no clouds, everything washed clean, a sharp whitish light so you couldn't tell where the sun was, and everywhere, excited, calling out to one another, were birds in the pine trees.

There was an old rotted doghouse or rabbit hutch I looked into behind the lodge but nobody was there, nor any sign of anybody.

When Momma was up finally and her face mottled and swollen with mosquito bites, her lip still swollen so she looked like somebody'd punched her with his fist, I told her about the little girls, I was talking fast and excited and Momma said, squinting at me like the morning light was hurtful to her eyes, "Honey, you were just dreaming, there aren't any other children here. Only you." I said, "Yes there are, Momma. I heard them, and I saw them." Momma went out into the kitchen where she tried to get the gas stove to light up so she could make coffee and I followed her repeating what I'd said, the girls were here some- where hiding I said, but Momma didn't pay too much attention to me. She was cursing under her breath looking for something then she found a box of wooden matches and with a shaky hand tried to light one, scraping it against a stove burner but the match must've been damp, the stick broke in her hand, she let the pieces fall to the floor and went to get her silver lighter Daddy'd given her out of her tote bag and that did work, a bluish flame flaring up at one of the burners with a hissing noise. I repeated what I said about the little girls, I'd seen them right outside by the front porch and they were sisters and they were crying because somebody was after them, it wasn't any God-damn dream I told Momma it was *not*. Bringing my bare heels down hard on the worn-out linoleum floor so the floorboards wobbled. Not minding how I was hurting myself till Momma slapped at me to quiet me.

I was like the gas burner flaring up, the blue flame going to orange if the gas's turned too high.

The others came in, Maude and Brownlee, and after a while we ate breakfast, some stale sweet rolls out of a package, and some mealy bananas, and the adults had coffee and smoked their cigarettes and I was telling them about the little girls I knew were somewhere at the camp, Momma kept trying to shush me but I wouldn't be shushed and there came a look into Maude's face and her eyes moved onto me for the first time like she hadn't seen me before. "What little girls are you talking about, Ingrid?" she asked. I said I didn't know their names, how would I know their names. I'd seen them in the middle of the night when everybody was asleep, out by the front porch they'd been, hiding in the grass, and crying. They were scared of something, I said. Like somebody was after them.

"What's this?" Maude asked, looking from me to Momma, and back again. "When was this?"

Maude was older than Momma by five or six years, heavier, with streaked brown hair tied up in a ker-chief, eyebrows plucked thin and arching like she was in perpetual surprise, and her bloodshot eyes too she was always widening to show surprise or interest or mockery. She was good-looking I guess but I didn't like her and for sure I knew she didn't like me. Earlier that morning I'd heard her and Brownlee curse each other because Brownlee was flying back to Marsena instead of staying with her the way she wanted. Now she was staring at me asking what did the little girls look like? and I tried to say but there weren't the right words, I was getting excited and picking at my mosquito bites and Momma took both my hands to calm me saying, "Ingrid, that's enough. Jesus, you had one of your dreams, that's all." But Maude was exhaling smoke in that slow watchful way of grown women, and she was looking at Brownlee, and Brownlee who hadn't been listening said, "What?" like he was pissed and Maude said, "Vaughn, she's talking about Earl Meltzer's little girls—that's who she's talking about. My God." Brownlee said, "She isn't talking about anything, she's just a kid making things up," and Maude said, shaking her head, her voice quick and scared, "She's talking about Earl Meltzer's little girls, there's nobody else she's talking about."

Now Momma set her coffee cup down. "Who's Earl Meltzer?—what is this?"

Brownlee was telling Maude, "She couldn't know about them, it was two-three years ago at least. So drop it. You're wasted from last night." But Maude was making these soft sighing scared-sounding noises to herself, fluttering her eyes, "Oh God, oh Jesus. She's seen them. Those poor little girls," and Momma said, "Maude? Vaughn? What the hell is this?" and Brownlee was telling Maude, "Look, somebody must've told her, that's all. She had a dream, that's all." Momma said,

"Tell her what, for Christ's sake?" Momma's eyes were sore-looking and her lip so swollen she hadn't even tried to put on lipstick like she always did, her skin looked dry as ashes in the morning light. Maude said, "Meltzer's little girls Cheryl and Doreen—*I* knew them! Meltzer and Lena his wife weren't living together, Lena was living with this other guy, in Watertown, and one night Meltzer went with a gun to get the girls from Lena's mother where they were staying, and he brought them out to the camp here, and—" and Brownlee cut her off saying, "Maude, shut the fuck up, you'll scare the kid," and Maude said, "*You* shut the fuck up, God damn you—you were a buddy of Meltzer's weren't you—thank God the prick put a bullet through his own brains too—"

Brownlee brought his opened hand around and hit the side of Maude's face, she screamed spilling hot coffee, and Momma screamed, and already I was running, out of the kitchen and through the back door where the screen was rusted and torn and I forgot I was barefoot running in the high grass around the side of the lodge, I wasn't crying because it wasn't me he'd hit, but I was scared, I crawled under the porch near where the girls had been and jays were screaming at me out of the pine trees and I pushed my way head-on through a rotted lattice covered in poison ivy and cobwebs till I was inside in this dark place smelling of something sharp crawling on my hands and knees and stones were stabbing me, pieces of glass, I was panting like a dog crawling halfway under the porch hearing how back in the kitchen they were still arguing.

Then it was quiet. It was still. Under the porch where the sun came through cracks in the floorboards in cobwebbed rays and there was this smell so sharp my nostrils pinched like something had died there, and old soft decayed leaves sticking to my skin, gnats buzzing in my face. And a mosquito whining, close by my ear. I knew to make myself as small as I could hugging my knees to my chest, hunched over so nobody could see if they came looking peering through the lattice. My right knee stung where it was bleeding but I wasn't crying. My hands were bleeding, too, but I paid them no mind. Momma's footsteps came quick overhead, I knew they were Momma's, so light and fast and then she was on the porch calling, "Ingrid? Honey, where are you?"

I waited like I knew to wait. I was used to hiding and some times I'd hidden nobody had even known I was gone, that was the safest kind of hiding and a principle to take to heart all your life.

So Momma didn't know where I was and she came down the porch steps talking to herself, muttering and cursing and I could see her legs, her legs in the white slacks, not clear but like I was seeing them through greenish water. Momma calling my name in that tight-scared way of hers so I knew if I revealed myself she'd be angry so I stayed where I was not making a sound.

I saw them then. At the farthest corner where it was darkest. The sisters crouched together in each other's arms. I saw their faces that were pale but smeared with something—dirt? blood? and I saw they were crying and they saw me, for a long time we looked at each other. "I'm an alive girl," I whispered. "I'm an alive girl not like you."

Marsena Sportsman's Club

You're a girl, Momma said. You're not one of them, they don't want you. You hear me?

I said Yes Momma. Never would I defy Momma if there was another way.

Only boys were hired at the Marsena Sportsman's Club. Boys from school, boys who lived on our road, nine-, ten-, eleven-year-olds hired to run out onto the shooting range or into nearby fields as far as the shot pigeons could fly. The idea was to kill them and *put them out of their misery*. The idea was to be *merciful*. Prevent the wounded pigeons from flopping around bleeding, a wing broken or an eye and a beak blasted away by buckshot. The boys were paid a quarter per bird to wring its neck, sometimes they'd twist the head right off, carry the limp body back to the range where the carcasses were dumped in a box.

Weekends were the busiest times. Summer through Labor Day.

We lived nearby. It was temporary Momma said. Ashamed of the place we rented because it was so shabby and Daddy was away and people would look at us so you'd know they were thinking certain thoughts they would not utter aloud. When Momma heard the gunfire start she'd press her hands against her ears and start to scream.

Crazy fools with their guns! Crazy bloodthirsty Goddamned bastards! How'd they like their own heads blown off, God damn them!

Girls weren't wanted but we'd hide in the bushes behind the club to watch. The times I remember most though are when I was alone.

First came the gunfire and the shouts making my head ring. Then the bird-shrieking and wing-flapping. It happened so fast!—some of the birds exploded in air, just feathers and blood, but others were able to keep flying, you couldn't believe how they'd keep flying, wounded like they were, wings flapping desperately ending up a mile away in somebody's yard or pasture or crash-diving against a window or in some woman's laundry hanging on the clothesline to dry— which happened one day to Mrs. Wicker living in a trailer next to our house. Mrs. Wicker was a fat young-ish woman who came out of her trailer screaming at Joey Cooper as he ran into her yard chasing a wounded pigeon, Joey boasted afterward he didn't slow up for a second just scooped up the pigeon where it'd dropped after striking a white cotton sheet, a sheet now blood-smeared hanging on the clothesline, and Joey wrung the bird's neck even as he turned running back in the direction of the club with Bonnie Wicker screaming at him all the while.

Not that it was bad as it sounds. Mr. Lovett the club manager paid for any *reasonable damage* an escaped pigeon caused.

This was *club policy*. This was *public relations*.

Breathless and hooting the hired boys had a great time. A quarter per bird was a lot of money. Four birds, $1. *One dollar!* The older more skilled boys like Joey Cooper, Lyle Stuckart who caught the most pigeons, outrunning the smaller boys or shoving them roughly aside, could make as much as $10 in a single day in summer, the range open till 10 P.M.

Nobody we knew from Marsena, nobody's father or grandfather or older brother we'd ever heard of belonged to the Marsena Sportsman's Club. Most of the members drove out from Yewville six miles upriver. They were businessmen, lawyers, doctors, men with money it was believed. They drove new-model cars, station wagons. They dressed well. Their guns were of high quality. In hunting season they gathered at the club then drove out into the country-side, sometimes they'd hire local guides. In season they shot squirrels, pheasants, white-tailed deer.

Weekends in summer gunfire at the club started early, as early as 9 A.M., and ended late. Like fire-crackers, or thunder. On Labor Day there was the Pigeon Shoot, not at the club because it was too big an event but in a farmer's pasture up the road. Hundreds of men and teenaged boys competing, cash prizes as high as $200 and because this was an open competi-tion, just an entry fee of $20 required, the winners were often from Marsena—once, Daddy's friend Vaughn Brownlee, another time Emory Boone who was a cousin of mine, only eighteen. Another time, Joey Cooper's grandfather.

The winners' pictures were taken and published in the *Yewville Journal*.

Why do they want to shoot pigeons? I asked
Momma and Momma said, They're men. It's what men
do when they can't shoot one another.

Just don't hang around that damned place, you
hear? Momma said. She'd look at me in that way of
hers, squinting against the smoke of her cigarette. You
promise?

My secret place was on a hill above the club where
there was underbrush, sumac and honeysuckle and wild
rose and a big fallen-over oak tree rotted and covered in
vines and stippled with toadstools that crumbled almost
to powder when you touched them. I could hide here
behind the tree and not be seen *like I was invisible*
and if a boy came running crashing through the underbrush yelling in pursuit of a wounded pigeon he'd never
see me.

Not once did one of them see me. I can dream of it
to this day and in my acid trips I'd be returned there,
that tree, crouching behind that tree, but I'd be flying
too, flapping my wings rising into the air in just that
instant before the *crack!* of the gun but the buckshot
would miss me, or pass through me. Rising to God,
feeling God's breath. That sharp smell of gunpowder.

Another thing I can see: in front of the club inside
the horseshoe driveway there was a tall metal flagpole,
a really tall flagpole you could see from a long distance. When the club was open, the flag was always up.
RED WHITE AND BLUE STRIPES blowing in the wind.

It was Joey Cooper I spied on when I could. Even
one day in a light drizzle, and another time, after a
storm the night before, in wet grass, mud. Joey was
eleven years old when I was eight, skinny and fast on

his feet as a young deer. He might've been any age, he seemed almost grown-up to me. Him and his brother Floyd I knew from school and from the bus we all had to take into town and back. The boys' mouths grinning, the words that flew from those mouths were *fuck*, *fucker*, *shit*, *cocksucker*, *suck*, *it sucks*, *it all sucks* and I would shape these words with my lips but never dared utter them aloud even to myself. Momma knew Joey's and Floyd's aunt but warned me to stay away from them, especially don't let them get you alone Momma said. No telling what kids like that might do.

Promise? Momma said holding my shoulders, stooping to peer into my eyes like she was trying to look into the future and I said, Yes Momma I promise.

Joey Cooper never knew my name nor gave me a second glance, I was too young, but I remember him, always I'll remember him, and the other boys, Floyd Cooper, Lyle Stuckart, a red-haired boy named Willy from the trailer court—their flushed sweaty faces lit up with smiles, fingers gripping lifeless birds, bloodied feathers.

Young, I knew not to expect mercy from such hands.

A Woman A Man Would Die For

Nothing like that river Momma loved. She'd been brought up near it in Shaheen and said it was like a big artery in her, gave her solace. So every time we moved it was to another town on the Chautauqua. From Marsena south twenty miles to Tintern Falls when Momma got restless. Some man, or men, troubling her. It was always men, and they were always trouble.

We were living by ourselves then, Daddy was away. And nobody would speak of him to me. And I never asked, for I knew *Never ask: If you are meant to know, they will tell you soon enough.*

It was the day after Easter Sunday 1975. Bright, windy and cold. Momma and I were coming from the post office on Main Street of Tintern Falls and it soon became apparent that a man was following us. No one Momma seemed to know. This was a thing that happened to Momma once in a while but always in a different way and with different consequences. And Momma's face was flushed and her mouth set and she refused to glance back at the man, the stranger, holding her head high and walking fast so I had trouble keeping up with her, my legs so short. It was a time when we didn't have a car. Or it was the old blue Chevy being repaired at a garage in town by a mechanic who was a friend of Momma's or a cousin of Daddy's or a man who owed Lucas Boone my father a favor. So we were reduced to walking, a mile and more across the Tintern Falls bridge to downtown and back again unless Momma called somebody to ask for a ride. Which she hated to do unless it was a ride to the women's clothing store where she worked four days a week and absolutely necessary *God damn I have my pride, my pride is about all I have.* And so there was Momma in her slim snug-fitting navy-blue bell-bottoms and a little greenish-plum velvet jacket she'd sewed for herself, blond hair like cornsilk blowing loose in the wind. And carrying her old taffy-colored leather bag beneath her arm because the strap is broken. And in the bag is a letter she'd snatched up out of her post office box and hid from my eyes and she will open it in secret in the bathroom of our rented second floor of a shabby woodframe house on Mill Street above the river, she'll read that letter in secret and immediately crumple and burn in the bathroom sink so the feathery gray ashes can be washed away down the drain and no trace remaining. *Momma what are you doing?* I will call through the door, anxious she's been in there so long, and the door locked against me and Momma will try to muffle her sobs saying sharp, angry *Nothing! Go away! Let me alone for five minutes for God's sake.*

But maybe the letter will have money in it. For afterward, saying it's a bonus from her boss, Momma will take me to the Sears Roebuck which is the big store in Tintern Falls, and buy me the new shoes I need in the children's shoe department. Or upstairs to the housewares department for an iron frying pan, an egg beater, a six-piece set of Fleur-de-lis stainless-steel flatware.

But now we're ten minutes at least from home. And there's this man in a fox-colored jacket, cigar clamped between his jaws, taller and heavier than Daddy, or my memory of Daddy, following Momma. On Main Street. Bright daylight, Monday near noon. This big staring man whose name Chloe Boone doesn't know but whose face might be familiar, sure it's possible he has been a customer buying for his wife, his mother, any female relative in Miss Ashley's Ladies Apparel which is one of the two or three most expensive stores in Tintern Falls, or in the Chautauqua Hotel lounge where Chloe Boone sometimes stops for just one drink on Friday afternoon, or in the Riverside Tavern where she goes some Saturday nights with a big gang of men and women her age, some married and some not—Tintern Falls is a small town of less than six thousand people. This man is keeping pace with us almost exactly like he doesn't want to scare us, like, just maybe, he's only walking in the direction we are; it's just coincidence. "Don't look back," Momma scolds, pulling me along. But I'm staring at this man the way he's staring at Momma and me, it's like when there's a dog trotting after you you can't stop yourself from glancing back to see is that dog wagging his tail hoping to be friends? or are his eyes glassed over, his hackles raised in meanness?—so I see this big nervously smiling man is nobody I've ever laid eyes on before in my life but the way he's watching my mother is a way I seem to know, I can feel the excitement of it, something forbidden, you're not supposed to do, anyway not on the street in public in broad daylight showing such raw need. And the excitement of it, sharp as pain, I can feel in the tightness in Momma's fingers around mine, it's coursing through her blood to mine for I am *Chloe Boone's daughter Ingrid. There was a baby boy of hers once but he went away, he wasn't loved enough. Only Ingrid remains and I am Ingrid and I know that I am pretty like Momma, my silky-curly pale hair, my brown eyes, everybody tells us so.* Is she your little girl? *men ask Chloe Boone smiling at the two of us looking from one to the other eating us up with their eyes in approval of what they see. For what men see is what we are.*

(Except: sometimes at night, wind-rocked nights when I wake up choking and trying to scream from a nightmare of flying in a rattly single-propeller plane that breaks to pieces high in the air. Daddy behind us at the pilot's controls and the helmet and plastic goggles on his head that isn't Daddy's head I remember but a grinning bony white skull, or if I'm sent home from school burning and dizzy with fever or bleeding from the itchy sores in my scalp and on my face and throat I can't help scratching, at these times Momma hugs me, rocks me in her arms like I was a tiny baby again and she's sobbing *What am I going to do with you, Ingrid! with you, I love you so much, and with me!* And we're alone at these times, and secret. And nothing of what anybody sees in us, none of Momma's men friends nor even Daddy himself if he was with us, is real.)

But now we're on Main Street of Tintern Falls. Passing Woolworth's, the Bridge Bar & Grill, McLain Shoes. There's traffic moving in a steady stream on the street, headed for and coming from the big high bridge. A Trailways bus marked *Yewville* where Momma took us once to see a man she called a lawyer, but later that day we went to the movies, saw *Paper Moon* I loved. There's that hard hurtful-white sunshine of windy days by the river, grit lifted from the pavement to fly into your eyes. And this man, this strange staring man in the fox jacket following us, who won't go away. Won't turn off into one of the stores, or decide to cross the street. He's older than Momma by a lot of years but has that kind of boyish-sly face, red-friendly face, a man used to getting his own way you can tell. A man following after a woman like it's his privilege, maybe in fact it's *her* drawing *him*, so who's to blame?

"Excuse me, ma'am—?"

He's tossed his cigar away into the gutter, he's smiling a big smile at last catching up with us as we're about to climb the stone steps to the bridge. And Momma can't avoid looking at him though she's still in motion, and still gripping my hand.

"Excuse me, ma'am: do you know the way to the nearest church?"

This brings Momma to almost a halt. She isn't prepared for this question.

"A *church?*"

"That's right, ma'am, can you help me?"

Momma's eyes are rising slow and unimpressed from the man's glary oxblood shoes to his face that's like a bright light beamed at her. Saying flat and cool, "Mister, any way would take you to a church, wouldn't it?—you keep going long enough."

The man presses his hand to his heart. His eyes are glistening and bulging a little, like marbles in his fleshy face. "Look, I need to get to a church *fast*. To fall on my knees."

Momma says, "Oh yes? Just why? Why's it so crucial?"

"Because I want to give thanks to God," the man says, like he's on TV or radio, making a statement, "—I'm looking at a woman so beautiful my heart is singing."

Momma bursts into laughter. That way she has, unexpected.

"You're an original, mister," she says, her eyes narrowed, assessing. "I hand you that."

The man laughs, pleased. There's a neat-trimmed fuzzy-blond mustache on his upper lip and his hair is faded blond, a tin color, his scalp showing through as the wind blows his lacquered hair and he's fumbling to stop it, to hold it in place, but too late. He's dressed to display he has money, and the taste to spend it right—the suede jacket opened on a bronze-shiny striped shirt and no necktie, sharp-creased dark trousers and the oxblood shoes the biggest shoes on the biggest feet I've ever seen, polished to a proud glare. Shows his big slightly crooked nicotine-stained teeth, says, "Yes ma'am. I guarantee you, I sure am."

"An original asshole."

It's like Momma has reached out and poked the man in the big belly of his swelling over his belt—a poke that's somewhere between a punch and a tickle, depending on how it's interpreted. He's laughing, his cheeks coloring. A man who's a good sport, I'm thinking he's almost handsome like a healthy hog would be handsome up on his hind legs and his eyes shining.

"Hell, I don't mind being an asshole, ma'am," he says, "—you're a woman a man would die for. But I'm more than an asshole, I hope you'll give me the opportunity to convince you?"

"No thanks."

"Hey: here"—he's taken something out of his inside pocket to give to Momma, his hand is bigger than both Momma's hands together, it's covered with bristly blond-tin hairs and there's a gold ring with a black stone gleaming on his smallest finger. It's a little white business card but Momma shrugs and ignores it, backing off, tugging at my hand again, "Ingrid, come *on*."

"You're not going to give me the opportunity to convince you?"

He sounds surprised, even a little vexed. Momma tosses back over her shoulder, not unfriendly exactly, but cool, on the edge of jeering, "Mister, I'm a woman requires a lot more convincing than you can provide."

So Momma is walking away. And me beside her, pulled along. There's a pedestrian walk on the left-hand side of the bridge, made of wood planks, and to get to it you have to climb crumbling stone steps, each step is so high I almost can't manage it and Momma is distracted not noticing because, behind us, the man is calling after her stubborn and confident, "Ma'am?—I sure disagree with you on that point. I'm a business-man and I know a good deal even when the good deal is *me* and I say, with all respect, ma'am, you're one hundred percent plain *mistaken*."

Momma mutters under her breath, "Asshole! Fuck off."

He isn't following us but still calls after, cupping his hands to his mouth, "Ma'am? You're not going to walk across that bridge are you?—in all this wind?"

Momma just pulls me along, not looking back. Her head high and proud and the taffy-colored leather bag tight under her arm.

* * *

Later he would say, confess he knew our names, of course. Knew where we lived, who we rented from. Knew Momma's marital situation, or anyway as much as the woman who was Momma's employer at the clothing store knew, which wasn't much. He would say he'd never in his life approached any woman in such a way, hoped to hell we believed him. But he couldn't help it: a woman a man would die for—*you don't meet that kind of woman every day.*

So we crossed the Tintern Falls bridge and left the man in the fox-colored jacket, the man with the staring eyes, behind. Forgotten. *I* forgot him.

Like Mrs. Prunty our third-grade teacher erasing the blackboard first with the eraser in slow measured swipes then with a wetted cloth, making the cloudiness go away, bringing a sharp dark shine to the board, I erased and forgot, erased and forgot, many things.

Things I saw in Nam Daddy used to say. That angry smile on his face. Shaking his head, shaking the sight of them out of his head like they were pieces of broken glass, erasing, forgetting, *You don't want to know.*

Always it was two times. The time that's *now* you're in, eyes wide open and seeing, and the time that's *past.* Some people, grown-ups, I believed, lived also in the *future.* But I could not.

Only the time that's *now* you share with other people.

Traffic passed us on the bridge and the bridge swayed harder, hummed and vibrated. The bridge at Tintern Falls is one of the bridges of my memory and that crossing, that day in the wind, is one of the crossings of my memory. My heart pounded like something was trapped inside it, thrashing its wings. My fingers gripped Momma's fingers tight, fearful she might slip away from me.

Always Momma stopped midway across the bridge to shade her eyes and look upriver where, a half mile away, the sixty-foot falls splashed and churned. If there was a rainbow, faint iridescent-transparent colors quivering out of the mist, she'd point it out, saying a rainbow is good luck, you can wish on a rainbow. *The first time your father took me up in an airplane it was a single-prop Cessna and we flew over the falls, so low I swear there was mist on the windshield* Momma would say, how many times she said, and each time was new to me, I wanted to hear more, more. Until one day it would be, must be, that Ingrid herself had been a passenger in that plane, squealing and breathless with excitement on that first, long-ago flight. *I swear there was mist on the windshield, the roar of the plane and the falls were all mixed together!*

It was a north wind, blowing in big scooping roaring gusts out of the mountains, following the course of the river it seemed, churning up water like the falls and the big rocks beneath. It should have been spring but the air tasted of winter. Even on sunny days the snow and ice had seemed reluctant to melt, like some white, grainy substance tougher and denser than mere water, but finally, the week before, it had melted, even in the darkest crevices of stone, and the Chautauqua River was high. Wild and fast in sinewy-snaky channels where if you stared you could see cloudy streaks of mud, froth, foam and debris, even dead animals or parts of them, mixed with the darker, clearer water. *Never know what you'll see in the river if you wait long enough!*—people said. Your own face drifting down far below in the dark water. A soul like foam, froth. Evaporating as the air touches it.

Like Time, too, is mixed. Separate channels of Time braided together and rushing past. You put out your hand to still it and it flows through your fingers like—water.

I ask Momma why can't you see the wind and Momma says because the wind is *invisible*, silly. Why is it *invisible?* I ask Momma and Momma laughs and pinches my cheek and says, because you can't *see* it. That look in her face, that's love.

Saying, "You can feel the wind, that's for sure. It can knock you on your ass quick enough. You don't need to see it, to know that simple fact."

It was since last November we'd been living in Tintern Falls, in the house on Mill Street. In this new school I was in, where I was quick and eager to make friends, and already counted I had five or six girlfriends, there was a cousin of mine named Mary Ellen Boone, a grade ahead of me, and not friendly. *Stay away from the Boones, we can't trust any of them* Momma said. Her face pinched and bitter in that way of hers that, if I asked any question, would just shut up tighter.

I knew, though, that the Boones, who were Daddy's relatives, did not get along with the McDiarmids, who were Momma's relatives. I seemed to know that they did not like Momma, and Momma surely hated them. But why, I didn't know. It might have seemed to me that there needed to be no reason.

"Momma, let's get off the bridge! Please."

"We will, quick enough. What's wrong with you?"

"I'm afraid."

"Oh, silly! Afraid of what? You're not going to fall in the river, Momma won't let you."

I was staring through the cracks between the big raw splintery planks. So loose-set you could see the water rushing below. After just a few seconds it would seem the bridge was moving, with you on it, and not the river! My insides shivered, like a little snake was wriggling inside.

"It's nice here," Momma said. She'd lit a cigarette, and that always made her dreamy. Smoke trailing out of her mouth and caught by the wind and blown away and she's picking a tiny piece of tobacco off her tongue, how well I remember that gesture, and the puckering of her forehead, the concentration. Waiting for what I didn't know to call *nicotine* to hit her veins, and her heart. That good sensation, that kick to the heart. Why do we love drugs, because they're so good for us, where's the mystery? I see Momma standing on that bridge halfway across between what they called the *downtown side* and the *mill side* and now I know why she had a habit of stopping there and staring upriver part smiling and part frowning and dreamy smoking her cigarettes, not wanting to continue on home, not wanting to be on land exactly, on one side or the other. Just there, on the Tintern Falls bridge. Where, her long blond hair blowing, her slender figure so striking in the plum-colored velvet jacket and the tight bell-bottoms, she'd be sure to attract the attention of anyone driving past. Men especially. But, back to traffic, she needed to see no one. Maybe she could pretend there was no one there.

Momma points out to me where sparrow hawks have nested in the highest girders of the bridge.

There's bird shit everywhere, streaking down the girders and encrusted on the wires and railings, once you
notice it you can't not see it: ugly. The Chautauqua
River is so wide here below the falls, the bridge needs
five concrete supports. It's a tall arched bridge, iron latticework, humming-vibrating wires fascinating to con-
template from shore. At both ends are rusted plaques
with Roman numerals that mean 1939, Momma says
ten years before *she* was born.

Momma smokes her cigarette and lets the butt fall
down into the water and turns finally and I'm tugging
at her hand, impatient to get across. At shore the river
is conspicuously shallower, muddier. Where we're
headed, the mill side, the northeast side, there are
enormous chunks of broken concrete sticking out of
the water, rusted pipes, twisted metal rods, debris
dumped into the river at the time the bridge was built,
so long ago, and never cleared away.

Kids weren't supposed to play anywhere along the
shore there, obviously it was dangerous. No wading in
the shallow water, and certainly no swimming.

I was a girl and girls weren't wanted. Except if I
played with other girls or boys my age or younger. The
big boys, the boys I admired, threw stones at us if we
ventured too close, snowballs or chunks of ice in winter. I'd run laughing and shouting as missiles pelted
around me, I'd turn boldly and stick out my tongue or
jerk my middle finger upward in that way the boys did
to one another, a gesture utterly mysterious to me, but
so potent! so amazing! drawing surprise, outrage,
attention. *That's all I want from them: to be seen.*

Once, Momma was never to know, it was the first
day of the thaw, a couple of weeks before Easter,

before the man in the fox jacket followed us, I was with some kids from Mill Street and we climbed down the riverbank to break off melting icicles and toss them into the river and some of the more daring of us made our way slipping and sliding across the broken concrete and rusted pipes to the underside of the bridge where when you looked up, it was such a surprise, you saw strange glimmering-ghostly reflections of the river, the rushing water, *the underside of the bridge was a skeleton of something not meant to be seen.* We cupped our hands to our mouths and shouted and the sound echoed the way the water-reflections seemed to echo and when it faded the noise of the river came louder than before. Birds nested on the rafters there, and in drainpipes, the older kids called them "river swifts" and they had sleek dark feathers, pale underbellies, forked tails, they were much smaller than the hawks, we tossed chunks of ice at them nowhere near hitting them. Their strange shrieking calls! Like they were cursing us, not knowing us. And one of the older girls pointed downriver past the train yard and the sour-smelling granary saying there's a swampy place where a few years ago a woman's naked body had been found and it was the woman's own husband who'd killed her, strangled her and dumped her body into the river up at Milburn and the river carried it all that way, over the falls, battering and hurting her so she was hardly recognizable. So it was said. Her own husband who was crazy for her and that's why it happened the way it did.

"Christ," says Momma, whistling through her teeth. "Some people don't give *up*."

Somebody's waiting for us on the other side of the bridge.

This gleaming Oldsmobile convertible lime-green and lighting up the air like a candle flame, parked, motor running, on the edge of the road just below the bridge ramp. A man standing there by the driver's opened door smiling at us with crinkled eyes—the man in the fox jacket, that fuzzy mustache on his lip!

I'm so surprised seeing him, I just stare. I'd erased him from my thoughts completely but here he *is*.

Momma doesn't seem surprised, much. Or impressed.

He's saying, "Excuse me, ma'am," more subdued now, looking at Momma like a cross word from her or even a mean glance would break his heart, "—but would you and your little girl accept a ride to wherever you're going?" and Momma just walks on, staring him down without a word, and quick and hopeful he continues, "Hmmm! Well, then I guess not—but here's my business card, ma'am—will you accept *this?* Never know when you might require some business expertise? . . ."

This time, for some reason, it's the way Chloe Boone is, quick and impulsive, unpredictable, she does take the card from the man's extended hand; and he blinks at her, touched, startled as if she has reached out and squeezed his hand. Just like that! He's almost stammering, "Ma'am, thank you, please call me anytime. You won't regret it, I promise."

Momma laughs, and drops the card into her bag without so much as glancing at it. Slips her arm around my shoulders, walking me past the Oldsmobile. Saying, coolly, with a shrug, "That's right, mister. I don't intend to regret anything."

You Trust
Your Daddy
Don't You

Daddy was gone. But lots of times he'd return to us from the sky. It would be night, and nobody around. An open field. Not one of the local airfields where people would know him, recognize him. Just an open field. Sometimes Momma was waiting with me but most often not. First the sound of the plane's motor louder and louder until it's inside you. A sensation in your chest tightening like a rubber band about to break. You open your eyes and there's the plane lowering out of the sky out of nowhere already landing—some two-seater Fairfield, or Cessna, or Stimson. Or was it the Vultee, the big Air Force trainer—propellers roaring like thunder. Daddy's already on the ground on his long legs coming fast to you, smiling, his arms opened for a hug. You want to run toward him but you can't. He takes off his dark-tinted flying goggles so you can see his eyes. But you can't see his eyes.

That dizzy whirring sensation of *motor*, *propellers*. Swallowing my mouth dry as chalk dust. Looking out the window craning my neck to see the sky. Ingrid, is something wrong? the teacher would ask. At home Momma would sigh laying her hand against my forehead. Shit, honey, you're burning up! Ice cubes wrapped in a towel against my face. Aspirin with orange juice. Made to go to bed early just a sheet covering me. Except I'd start to shiver sometimes, my teeth chattering. Momma's voice over the phone talking to her man friend low and worried—she'd use her excuse, her excuse Mr. Zink couldn't budge. Ingrid's sick, Ingrid's got a fever, sweetie. You'd better not come over tonight, O.K.?

Daddy had never taken me up in the Vultee trainer with the sliding-canopy open cockpit like he'd promised. But by the age of ten I'd gotten to the point where I could remember that flight as well or better than the flights in the smaller planes he'd actually taken me on and drew the plane and Daddy and me in it a hundred times and once on a sheet of construction paper the size of my desktop at school, such a good crayon drawing my teacher tacked it up on the bulletin board soaring above the other children's drawings and there it remained for a long long time. Every morning I entered homeroom—this was fifth grade, Tintern Falls Elementary—my eyes would fly to the bulletin board just to the left of the door, to the drawing, Daddy and me in the Vultee trainer with the canopy missing and the propellers ingeniously blurred to show speed. Blue streaks in the background that was the sky, no sign of land at all. I'd boast about flying in the Vultee and even the boys were impressed. When they asked why was the pilot in the rear seat not in the front I said laughing a little in derision they were so ignorant, Because that's how it is! An airplane isn't a car. I could talk about flying in the Vultee to Lake Ontario, to Niagara Falls where Daddy flew so low we could see the falls as close as you can see the Tintern Falls from the bridge, and people were gaping up at us, and waving. If Momma overheard me bragging to neighbor kids she'd call to me to come inside and scold, Daddy never took you up in that plane, that was me, and we didn't buzz Niagara Falls, you'd better believe it! Don't make up stories, sweetie. I was astonished, it was a surprise worse than being slapped, more hurtful. Goddamn yes he *did* I told Momma, Daddy did he *did*. And thinking of it now it's easy as shutting my eyes I remember Daddy lifting me in his strong arms up onto the Vultee's wing so I can climb into the cockpit, I remember Daddy strapping me in, his big smile as he puts on his dark-tinted goggles and adjusts the strap under his chin, then climbing back into the cockpit close behind me and continuing to talk to me happy and excited as a boy raising his voice to be heard over the terrible roar of the propellers, laughing telling me not to be afraid honey, this is the safest plane of them all 'cause it's an Air Force trainer. You trust your daddy don't you?

See You in
Your Dreams

That first time, it was noon recess at school. A blowy autumn day. I was sitting on a bench in the playground with two other fifth-grade girls eating our lunches out of paper bags and this man appeared and stood watching us from about ten feet away. There was a rusted old chain-link fence at the edge of the playground but you could slip through it, the man must've come in that way. Tall and dark-haired, a stylish-looking sport coat and a dark blue shirt open at the throat, aviator sunglasses so greeny-dark his eyes were hidden. He was so handsome! Standing there, like he'd been watching us for some time, and smiling. When I looked up he said, "Ingrid? Hey: Ingrid Boone." His smile widened. I stared at him and I knew who he was though I had not seen him in a long time. My heart stopped and when it started again I was on my feet, I'd dropped my lunch bag and he had my hand tight in his and we were walking fast to his car parked at the edge of the playground, the motor running.

I whispered, "Daddy? Daddy?" squinting up at him so hard it hurt and Daddy said, a finger to his lips, "Uncle Jack, let's say. Uncle Jack Boone, baby."

* * *

Five times in all, October–November 1977 when I was ten years old and Momma and I were living in a rented house in Tintern Falls, and Daddy came to see me in secret. Just that once at noon, it was too risky at noon. The other times he'd be waiting for me after school in his rented car. Driving out along the river into the hills, north of town we'd be parallel with the Chautauqua & Buffalo train tracks elevated above the river on a wooden trestle then disappearing into the tunnel at Block Hill. That tunnel!—a gouged-out hole like a nightmare in the side of the earth. The way even on the sunniest day light could penetrate the hole only a short distance then ceased as if the darkness was an actual substance, a barrier that could stop it. I'm dreaming of it all these years.

I was excited and scared believing that Daddy would drive us both away, we'd fly away and be hidden together, but each drive came to an end. Daddy crossed the river at Milburn, or Flemingville, or Shaheen. Driving back to Tintern Falls where he'd let me off a half mile from the clapboard house on North End Avenue where Momma and I lived not needing to ask me, the first day, where it was we lived.

Saying, "Walk straight home now, baby. And don't look back."

Every time I looked back, from the walk to our house, Daddy's car would be gone.

Daddy warned me not to tell Momma, this was our secret and if I told he might have to go away again and I would never see him again.

I loved Momma, it was like Momma and I were the

same person sometimes and she did know my secrets but not this one. I told Daddy I would die before I told anybody and Daddy laughed and said that wasn't necessary but it was flattering to hear.

Momma took pride dressing up in high heels, stockings, floral-print dresses she'd sewed herself or filmy blouses and tight straight skirts, Momma owned a dozen belts of leather, linked metal, shiny plastic to show off her slim waist where she worked as "receptionist" at Zink's Real Estate & Home Insurance on Front Street, downtown. Sometimes she didn't get home till after 6 P.M. weekdays. There were times even later on Friday. Or I'd look out the living-room window past the scrawny bamboo growing wild in the front yard and there Momma would be sitting with Mr. Zink in his lime-green Oldsmobile at the curb the two of them talking, laughing or frowning or arguing with the earnestness of men and women on TV you watch in close-up who can't see you in turn.

So if I was late coming back from school Momma wouldn't know and whatever she'd ask me I would reply as Daddy instructed as if Daddy hadn't ever been in town. I'm the invisible man, Daddy said, kissing my forehead. I'm just passing through.

Daddy spoke of Florida—Tampa, Miami, Key West. The Gulf of Mexico. He was a freelance pilot now, he made good money flying light cargo and sometimes passengers in the Caribbean. Journeys by night, squalls and thunderstorms. A forced landing once on a mile-long nameless island west of Jamaica. Daddy's southernmost destinations were Caracas, Venezuela, and Bogotá, Colombia. He spread out badly wrinkled maps to show me but the maps were discontinuous and I had no idea how far away these places were from Tintern Falls, New York. A long long way Daddy said touching the tip of his finger to my nose. Much of it over shark-infested waters.

Another thing Daddy would say mysteriously, folding up his maps to fit into his pocket, was there's nowhere in the human world you can't fly to if you've got enough fuel in your tank.

Daddy's wallet was like no other wallet I'd ever seen—made of crocodile hide, in shiny patches. There was a look of pride to it, so thick with bills it couldn't be snapped shut.

A $1 bill Daddy gave me, slipping into my pocket. Another time a $5 bill. Warning me not to spend it so anyone would be suspicious. Above all it was to be a secret from Momma—O.K.?

Snapshots Daddy carried in that wallet, years old and beginning to tear. Laying them out carefully like playing cards, like a game of solitaire, on the picnic table behind the Tastee-Freez. I was spooning chocolate ice cream into my mouth and the spooning slowed as I stared at the snapshots. "Who's that!" I snorted with derision pointing at a little girl about two years old with filmy blond curls, big round eyes catching two points of light that made them look like cat's eyes, or something radioactive. "That's you," Daddy said, annoyed. "Who else's beautiful baby girl am I gonna carry in my wallet, except my own?" There was a snapshot of Momma so young and beautiful in cutoff jeans and a red halter top holding a baby up beside her face, I stared and stared jealous of that baby! And Momma and Daddy so young in some time I didn't know long ago, arms linked tight around each other's waist, good-looking and arrogant preening themselves for the camera—they might've been certain of the young people my eyes snagged on in Tintern Falls and followed in the street.

Daddy tapped that snapshot with his finger, the nail of which was blackened from some injury. "Here's the start of it," he said, smiling hard. "That can't be erased."

I liked best a picture of Daddy in his zip-up flying jacket and Momma with his Navy pilot's cap cocked on her head and me, Ingrid, about seven years old, the three of us looking like a family you might recognize as such. We were standing in front of the Waco with the glitzy gold-painted wings at the Marsena airfield. I remembered that sporty airplane I hadn't seen for years and I started to cry and Daddy looked sad and told me not to cry, baby, it was going to be O.K.

Daddy's dark brown hair was cut shorter now. There were vertical dents in his cheeks like lines made with a ruler. He was two or three days unshaven. Tears came into his eyes easily, he'd wipe them away with the edge of his hand. In a paper bag in his coat pocket there was a pint bottle of whiskey he'd take a small quick swallow from then replace like it wasn't there. Still he dressed well, he was a good-looking man and he carried himself with pride. You could see he'd been a Navy pilot or somebody in the armed forces who'd worn a uniform. I noticed how men's eyes lighted on him hoping they knew him, he'd call out hello and slap their arms. Women's eyes trailed after him. At the Tastee-Freez the woman at the screened counter smiled at Daddy flirting trying to start a conversation, her gaze running over him like warm water and spilling onto me. Saying, "I love your little girl's hair, wish mine was that color!" and Daddy said, "Thanks, this is my little niece," and the woman said, "Uh—d'you live around here, mister?" and Daddy said, politely, backing off, "Fact is I don't, ma'am, sorry," and the woman persisted raising her voice to call after, "I was just trying to decide if you looked sort of familiar or not," and Daddy laughed and said, "Maybe you've been seeing me in your dreams?"

This was another thing I hadn't told Momma.

At Tintern Falls Elementary School there were cousins of mine bussed in from the country Momma warned me not to mix with any more than I needed. Blood kin of mine, not hers—they were Boones.

The oldest was Mary Ellen Boone in sixth grade. A fat-faced girl with mean eyes. She'd watch me at recess and after school and one day brushed against me, bumped me on the playground and said, in a low voice, like this was something her mother had warned her against too, "Your daddy is a *wanted* man, your daddy is *in trouble* with the law!" I stared at her in astonishment and she said it again in a louder thrilled voice, "Your daddy is a *wanted man!* Your daddy is *in trouble* with the law! He's gonna go to jail if they catch him!" I said, "You're a liar!" and she said, "*You're* a liar!" I shoved her, and she shoved me back. She smelled like a hog on a hot wet day. I punched her on the shoulder and she punched me in the face and kids were gathered around us laughing and yelling, I backed off and ran away furious my face hot with tears.

* * *

If I could open a vein. Not to inject any shit, I will never weaken like that again, but just to feel the kick of it, the old memory. So this numbness lifts. So I could get back there easier.

Tell me of your life you said.

I don't know my life. I have learned certain facts.

In fall 1977 when he returned to Eden County as a *wanted man*, my father Lucas Boone was thirty-three years old. Chloe Boone my mother, still his wife, though they had lived apart for almost five years, was thirty. They'd been married in 1966 in the country town of Shaheen in a Luthern church to which Chloe's family, the McDiarmids, belonged, though neither Lucas nor Chloe were believers. *If there could be a God* my father said *what would he care about us? It's to make something of yourself, pretending God gives a damn.* But this was good-natured talk, joking. And Momma laughed and kissed him *I think that's a great idea, what's wrong with that? Let's make something of ourselves we weren't before. Let's be happy!* Their first baby was born ten months after the wedding, a boy who died of meningitis at the age of five weeks and was buried in the Lutheran cemetery close by the graves of the McDiarmids. *So bitter in his heart* it was said of Lucas Boone *he would not mourn. He would not cry. Would not speak of it, nor visit the little grave.*

The second baby was a girl, born on December 11, 1967, in Port Oriskany, and this baby they believed would live and so they gave her a name: *Ingrid.*

In June 1968 Lucas Boone, a young father of only

twenty-four, joined the Navy to serve in Vietnam. He was Airman First Class Boone when honorably discharged in January 1971. He returned with assorted medals that soon came to be misplaced, lost. He did not speak easily of the war and of the distant country of Vietnam, as distant to the inhabitants of rural Eden County as another planet, he did not speak except to say that it was "beautiful." There was a surprised tone to his voice, a look in his face of incomprehension and subtle resentment as of one affronted by an insoluble riddle. In the early and mid 1970s Lucas Boone and his wife and little girl lived for a while in rented housing in Port Oriskany, and in Shaheen, and in the countryside near Marsena. Details of his employment during this time are vague. He flew single-prop planes for Mohawk Air in the Great Lakes region, he worked in the Allis-Chalmers plant in Port Oriskany. He drove a truck for a gravel company. He became a foreman for a lumberyard. He was often gone for days, sometimes as long as a week. In August 1977 a warrant was issued by the Port Oriskany police for Lucas Boone's arrest: he was one of five men wanted for questioning in the shooting death of an alleged drug dealer in Port Oriskany. In time the other four men were arrested and interrogated and all but one wound up in Red Bank State Prison for Men and that one was a close friend of Lucas Boone's named Vaughn Brownlee who was shot dead by an unknown assailant or assailants in a street in Port Oriskany in September 1977. Lucas Boone, who'd disappeared immediately following the shooting of the drug dealer, had never been located by police, never arrested.

These are facts. Except for the date of my birthday, I

would not have known any of them in the fall of 1977. For children know nothing factual about their parents or about their own lives.

Facts are the last thing you learn about your family. By the time you learn, you're no longer their child.

Like a small plane in bad weather circling a field to land but fearful of coming in so at the last minute nosing up, regaining altitude and recircling, my father circled the subject of my mother, fearful of confronting it head-on. Smoking his Camels, uncapping and sipping from his pint of Four Roses. Smell of smoke in the car's interior, sweet-sickish smell of whiskey. Daddy's oiled hair. And a new suede jacket he'd just bought himself, now the weather was turning cold, hadn't brought many clothes up from Florida with him—that smell of suede, rich red-brown of a deer's summer coat. My nostrils widened greedy and hopeful.

How many times saying, as if he was arguing, pleading his case, with someone not present, "*You* know I love you, Ingrid, don't you?—been missing you, and your Momma, like crazy." And, "Hope you forgive your dad being away so long?" He'd run his hairy-knuckled fingers over his face, digging at his eyes like he wanted to tear away some sight, or memory. Saying, in an undertone, "It isn't like I had much choice."

Shy I'd murmur Yes Daddy.

Shy, eager. *Yes* Daddy.

The answer that's required. The only answer.

Bringing quick easy tears into the man's eyes, bloodshot worried eyes. That spark like a match flaring up.

So he'd say next he'd make it up to me someday—
"You and your momma both."

He'd say, exhaling smoke like it was poison, angry-
eager to get it out of his lungs, "In the meantime this is
our secret, baby. Just you and me. Right?"

Secrets have always been easy for me, it's the opposite of *secrets* that is hard.

Till one November afternoon parked in the car,
Ford compact dull dishwater-brown to attract no
one's suspicious eye, we were off the highway north of
Tintern Falls above the river that was coarse and
choppy in the wind, and the sky like an enamel table
that's been scratched and the dark underside's
showing through, and we heard a train whistle, and
sat in silence staring at a locomotive and freight cars—
I counted thirty-two—CHAUTAUQUA & BUFFALO—
BALTIMORE & OHIO—NEW YORK CENTRAL—thunder
past on the wooden trestle that didn't look substantial
enough to support them and disappear into the
tunnel in Block Hill like a snake disappearing into a
hole and the deafening-rattling noise of the freight
cars too was sucked away with such suddenness it was
like there had never been any train, any noise, at all.
That's how you die: are gone. That fast.

It wasn't my thought but Daddy's. I heard it as if
he'd spoken it aloud.

And suddenly Daddy said, "This Zink. This friend of
your momma's. Tell me about him."

It should have been a surprise to me, Daddy knew
about Mr. Zink. But I understood he would know, like
he'd known where we lived without asking, and
where I went to school.

Shy I said, "I don't know. . . . He's O.K."

"He's married, eh? He's got some family some-where, eh?"

This I didn't know, this left me blank. Staring down at my hands in my lap that wanted to twist, writhe like something trapped.

Daddy uncapped the bottle of Four Roses and seemed to be weighing it in his hand before taking a quick swallow. Not looking at me like his questions shamed him. "Your momma—she likes Zink, eh?" he asked, and I shrugged and murmured I guess so, and he asked, "Does this guy pay for the house? Does he *own* the house?" and I said I didn't know, such a question was a surprise to me. Daddy asked, "Does he bring you things?—presents?" and I nodded yes, and he asked, "What? What's he bring you?" and I told him a doll I hated, a record player, a game called Sorry, angora mittens, and my voice faltered so Daddy asked, "And your momma, what's he bring her?" and I said stammering what came into my head, a TV, a toaster, a pair of leather boots, helped pay for the car, and going to the dentist, and again my voice faltered so Daddy broke in, "He comes over a lot, eh? How many times a week?" and I stared at my hands in my lap, I couldn't stop my fingernails from digging against my thumb-nails where the quicks were already scabby, I shook my head I didn't know, and Daddy asked, "Once? Twice? Three times? Every fucking night?" and I shook my head I didn't know, and Daddy asked, "Does he stay the night, sometimes?" and again I shook my head, and Daddy asked in this patient voice you'd use to speak to a dumb little kid, "Look: is he there in the mornings sometimes?—'Maynard Zink'!" and I was getting scared, a memory came to me now of Daddy angry, Daddy reaching out and shoving Momma, and Momma screaming, I stammered and said no, I didn't think so—no. Daddy took a swallow of his whiskey, and was quiet for a minute, then said, in a careful voice, looking at me, "Baby, either Zink is there, in that place you live, in the mornings sometimes, or he isn't. You'd know, right?—unless you were blind and deaf."

Not Mr. Zink but some other men sometimes—younger men, men more Momma's age, one of them named Randy with his hair in a ponytail who was a bartender in town and rode a motorcycle and called me Toots I specially liked, these men might stay the night with Momma sometimes. But not Mr. Zink.

Shook my head trying not to cry, the angry sound of Daddy's voice and the jeering in it, like the jeering of the older boys at school for any of us, girls—so hurtful it was like I'd been slapped.

Daddy muttered, "O.K., baby. What you don't know, you don't know." He drained the last drop of the whiskey and lowered the car window and tossed the bottle down the embankment into the water and said like he was making a decision, or had already made it, "All it comes down to in life, Ingrid, a man wants to do the right thing. I want to be a good man." He paused, and rubbed again at his eyes. "I know I made mistakes, I made a wrong turn. It isn't in my heart, or in my nature, y'know—like a scorpion has a nature?—a copperhead snake?—to be a good man. But I think I can go against my nature. Do you think that's possible, Ingrid?"

I said I didn't know. I was nervous and scared and

now one of my hands was loose, my fingers jammed into my mouth.

Daddy said, like he was arguing with somebody not visible, "I want to be a decent person. I've got a chance now, I've got money saved and I can begin again. It's just that I can't see any good reason not to be a bastard. I was trained young, and the training took. Blowing off guys' heads—it settles any doubts you have about them, or them about you. And like I say, it's my nature."

I asked, scared, "You aren't going to blow off Mr. Zink's head, are you Daddy?"

Daddy squinted at me and laughed, turning down one side of his mouth like he'd done with the flirty woman at the Tastee-Freez. "You think I should, baby?"

And even then I think now he didn't know what he intended to do. Why he'd come back, what he wanted. I'd believed he had a plan from the first like a pilot would make charting a course to fly but I was a child and could not have understood how even adults, even my father Lucas Boone might be walking through their lives not knowing where they were going and what they wanted or even told themselves they wanted as in a story with a destination. It was more Daddy was a man playing solitaire, slapping down the cards to see how they fell, how the game shaped up. You could always sweep the fucking cards away, or you could continue playing and win. If Daddy had a map of the possibilities before him in his head it was a map of mostly emptiness. Like the turquoise sea called *Caribbean*.

That map that's torn and folded a thousand times, that map I stole from him.

It was so. Maynard Zink who was Momma's employer, her boss she called him teasing to his face, dropped by our house on North End Avenue two-three times a week. Never weekends. Momma sometimes invited him to stay for supper and he'd blink at her like he'd never expected such a thing. "Are you sure, Chloe?" he'd ask, rubbing at his mustache. "You've got room for a big lug like *me?*"

The kind of man who, every time he steps through a doorway, he's squinting anxious to see if he's welcome. Even when the doorway is his own.

Momma spoke of Mr. Zink as the kindest man she knew. Saying to her women friends he was a sweetheart, not a stingy bone in his body. How it was between him and his wife she didn't know and she didn't want to know, that wasn't her business. Sure, Maynard Zink was a bit of a fool but that's the only kind of man you can trust. Saying, "Christ knows, I've had enough of the other kind."

Piggy-Zink I called him in secret. Though I liked him, I liked him because he liked me. Brought me presents, looked at me and listened when I spoke, answering his questions that were polite but also sincere. He was a tall slope-shouldered man many years older than Momma but not so old, Momma liked to say, as he appeared. That kind of fair thin wind- or sunburnt-looking skin that flushes easily. His belly was the size of a honeydew melon balanced above his belt. His faded-yellow hair was combed in thin separated strands across his forehead, and his eyes were shrewd and damp and eager and mournful all at once. Some nights Momma or I might see him driving past the house slow and cruising in his green Olds and we'd laugh at him, other nights we'd feel sorry for him and Momma would send me out onto the porch to wave him inside. You wouldn't know, Momma said, Maynard Zink had the money he had.

Crazy for Chloe Boone. So he'll take all kinds of shit.

I'd hear them talking quietly, laughing out in the living room when I was in bed and supposed to be asleep. The clink of bottles, glasses. Mr. Zink liked to eat, and he liked to drink—bringing six-packs of ale, gallon bottles of Chianti, his favorite Kentucky bourbon. Sometimes they did quarrel, it's true. Or Momma spoke sharply or dismissively to Mr. Zink, and Mr. Zink grunted and laughed a little like a boxer taking a blow to the gut. That big a man, big-bellied lug, he could absorb a woman's punches couldn't he? And beg for more?

One night I woke hearing what sounded like Momma sobbing. Unless she was laughing. A drunk-shrieky sound, then whispering and silence. Not in the living room, the lights were out when I checked, but next door in her bedroom. *Piggy-Zink! He's in there.* There was no light beneath Momma's door so they were in there in the dark. I heard the bedsprings, and more whispering. We'd only been living in the clapboard house on North End Avenue a few weeks, a furnished bungalow Mr. Zink called it, but already I was waiting for Daddy to come through the front door. He'd land his plane in a field nearby and he'd come to the house and he wouldn't knock, he wouldn't open the door as you open a door, it would fly open before him, shattering. There would be his fierce angry eyes, and his fists. There would be his gun.

A tickle between my legs in that soft secret sliver of flesh between my legs I had no name for, sharp and sudden. Remembering that gun that fitted in my daddy's hand. That, other times, I forgot.

That night, Daddy did come to the house. Momma opened the door, and there he was. The two of them staring at each other while Maynard Zink in the living room, in his undershirt, called out, "Who is it, Chloe?—anything wrong?"

It was just past 11 P.M. I was asleep in my bed at the back of the house and I woke terrified hearing their voices, raised and excited.

I ran to see, and Momma was trying to pull the men apart. It happened that fast. Momma barefoot in jeans and a tight black rib-hugger sweater looking like a high school girl except her face was dead-white and her mouth red like something pasted on her skin. She was crying, "Luke! My God, Luke! No—" and Daddy was saying, "I'm here to speak with my wife *alone*," leaning his face toward Mr. Zink's, "—you got that, mister?—get out of here!" and Mr. Zink scared and clumsy like a man in a dream not knowing what's happening except it's happening too fast for him to comprehend, saying, "See here!—see here!—" and Daddy shoved Mr. Zink with the flat of his hand, and Mr. Zink stumbled against a table and a lamp overturned and Momma screamed, but Mr. Zink didn't fall, it may even have been that Daddy grabbed his arm to keep him from falling. Mr. Zink wheeled upon him, a strand of hair loose across his forehead and his big face flushed, his mouth pursed like a baby's, Mr. Zink flailed with his fists but landed no blows because Daddy slipped them snakelike and agile and laughing. Daddy was wearing his new suede jacket, and his dark oiled hair gleamed, he was smiling, angry but smiling, no dark glasses now so his face looked rawer and more exposed and you could tell he'd been drinking, there was that heated flush to his cheeks. "I said, I'm here to speak with my wife, asshole, so get out," Daddy said. Mr. Zink was puffing, teetering on his clumsy legs, I was ashamed of him, embarrassed, his melon-belly so prominent in his undershirt, his flashy checked trousers riding low on his hips like a young guy's except Mr. Zink wasn't young. He stood taller than Daddy but slope-shouldered, his fatty chest rising and falling, confused in his body while Daddy was quick and purposeful as an upright snake. Daddy said, contemptuously, "Out! Out of here before you get hurt, 'Zink'! Think I don't know *you*, I know *you*, 'Zink'! Bastard! Cocksucker! Taking advantage of another man's wife because she needs money, 'Zink'! Think I don't know *you?*" and Mr. Zink was mumbling, panting, "See here!—just a minute!—I don't care who you are, m-mister!—you have no right—" and Daddy pushed at him backing him up and Momma pulled at Daddy's arm pleading, begging like I hadn't seen her in years. Remembering now: Momma pleading with Daddy, Daddy a force like flame, a column of fire, dangerous just to touch, ready to flash, to strike, in any direction. Daddy didn't push Momma aside, he was gentle with her, even as she slapped at him, screamed and wept calling his name, he wasn't even looking at her nor did he see me cringing in the doorway. A man only looks at another man in such a situation and he was looking at Mr. Zink contemplating what to do. This middle-aged paunchy fool who wouldn't back down from Lucas Boone! Like Maynard Zink didn't even know who Lucas Boone was.

Then something shone in Daddy's face. He leaned in, and punched the other man in the face in short stinging jabs, not hard, as if to demonstrate what he could do, what Mr. Zink wheezing and puffing, now dripping blood from his nose down onto his undershirt, couldn't prevent him from doing. Momma gave a sharp hurt cry at the sight of the blood. "Luke, no! Please, Luke!—let him go!" and Daddy said, in almost a level, normal voice, "The bastard can go, Chloe, any time he wants to." But Mr. Zink didn't back down from Daddy—that was the strange, the unexpected thing. You wanted to scream at him to get out, to escape, but he was trying to push himself at Daddy, so many years older than Daddy and so badly out of condition, his eyes popping in their sockets, a big vein like a worm throbbing in his forehead. He was muttering, "God damn you, mister! You can't just do these things! *You* bastard!" Daddy hid his surprise saying, "C'mon, shit-head! Think you can do it, eh?" now teasing Mr. Zink lowering his fists so that the older man could hit him if he could catch him but Daddy was too quick, leaping to the side, ducking and dancing backward, and Mr. Zink wild-eyed swung his big balled fists first the right then the left missing Daddy, then stumbling in pursuit of him and, almost falling into him, striking a clumsy blow on Daddy's raised forearm. Daddy was saying, teasing, "Maynard Zink! Fucking another man's wife! Think you can do it, eh?" Daddy leaned his face toward

Mr. Zink and Mr. Zink swung again blindly striking
Daddy above the eye, Daddy laughed, steeling himself
to be hit, goading his opponent into hitting him, there
was a flurry of ill-coordinated blows but Daddy didn't
flinch or back away though now his face was too shiny
with blood and Momma was pushing Mr. Zink away,
sobbing, "Stop it! Maynard! God damn *you!*" Still
Daddy kept it up, taunting Mr. Zink, " 'Maynard'! Fuck-
face! Cocksucker! She's my wife and this shit with you
it's just for what she can get out of you, asshole!"—
laughing now, grunting and laughing as he presented
himself to Mr. Zink who punched at his chest, his
stomach, wincing as he struck Daddy's belt buckle
with his bare fist. Momma slapped at Mr. Zink screaming, "I said stop! Stop! You're crazy as he is! I hate
you!"

The men ceased. Like baffled animals, breathing
hard, unable to catch their breaths, their chests rising
and falling. Their faces were slick with blood, perspira-
tion. Their clothes were splattered with it. Mr. Zink in
his stained undershirt, the white elastic band of his
undershorts showing above the waist of his trousers,
his right eye beginning to swell, looked like an old
man, dazed, ravaged, swaying on his feet on the verge
of collapse. Daddy, holding himself erect and arrogant
as a fighting cock, was panting too, swiping at his
bleeding eye as if he didn't know what had happened,
he too was dazed, his face reddened from the blows
he'd absorbed. And Momma sobbing as if her heart
was breaking—backing off from him when he reached
to her.

The living room that had been so cozy, this room
Momma and I had loved, was a shambles like a tor-

nado had raged through. The glass-topped table over-turned, the sea green ceramic lamp broken, a half dozen ale bottles and glasses on the floor, ale spilled and pungent-smelling soaking into the carpet, the rust-colored shag carpet Momma and I had bought at a discount store in town. There were bright red splashes of blood on the sofa, on the floor, even on the nearest wall. On a farther wall Momma had hung a mirror framed in black-lacquered wood in a style meant to be Oriental and this mirror was crooked and seemed to be reflecting a crooked, drunken scene. I stood in the doorway in my pajamas blinking not knowing what I saw but feeling that unmistakable aftermath of a fight, that thrill, that wild thrum in the nerves, the pulse that's still in the air, agitating the air like ripples in water. Like that heavy sweet-pounding blood-beat after you've come, somebody has made you come, and you didn't know what it was or how badly you wanted it until now.

Then Momma turned, and saw me at last. Murmuring "Ingrid!"—her eyes swollen and brimming with tears, and she came to me and hugged me so tight it hurt and both of us trembling and I wasn't crying, I was terrified but I wasn't crying. Because this had happened before and it would happen again how many times it would happen again and no one could stop it nor would wish to stop it despite the words that are uttered, the guilty eyes, the shame. Momma was framing my face in her hands, my face that was feverish, "Honey, go back to your room, will you? It's all right, honey, nobody's hurt, nobody's going to hurt you but you shouldn't be here, you shouldn't be up so late seeing such things."

And Daddy said, angry, like he was ashamed, "Do like your momma says, Ingrid."

Momma pushed me toward the door and I retreated into the shadowy hall and I heard Momma say, "Oh my God. This is what I deserve isn't it. This is what I deserve."

But already Daddy was speaking with Mr. Zink again. It was as if a veil had been drawn over me and I was invisible, they forgot me at once.

Daddy was saying, "Chloe is my wife, Zink! Got it? She's my wife you've been fucking, and it's over now, so get out of here!" and Mr. Zink fumbling to wipe his face with a wadded tissue, dropping the tissue and unable to retrieve it, stared blinking at Momma and for a long moment his mouth worked, he couldn't speak, then he said in a weak, plaintive voice, "Chloe? Dear? Is it so? You want me to leave?" and Momma said, "Yes. Please. You'd better, Maynard. He'll hurt you if you don't," and Mr. Zink said, "Should we call the police? Chloe?" and Momma said quickly, "No! Not the police. Just leave, please," and Mr. Zink said, groping toward her, blinking and baffled, "*You* want me to leave, Chloe? Leave you and Ingrid here with this—madman?" Trying to touch Momma's arm and she threw off his hand with a look of repugnance, a gesture so quick and instinctive there was no mistaking what it meant, and Momma cried, "Yes! Please! For Christ's sake *go!*" but still Mr. Zink groped toward her like a blind man, his eyes bleary and bloodshot, he stammered, "Chloe? You c-can't mean it!— This house— You promised—" and Momma turned on him now furious, as if she was ashamed Daddy was a witness to this exchange, "Go away, I told you! Don't touch me! You disgust me!" and Mr. Zink

stood swaying staring at her and I saw in his face the
look I'd seen that first time he'd followed Momma in
the street, drawn to the promise maybe of what was
mean and pitiless in her, Momma saying, "Luke is right.
He's always right. I'm only here, with you, for what I can
get out of you. That's the only reason. If you weren't
such a fool you'd know. Now get out!"

So it ended like that. Mr. Zink was panting like a
wounded animal but he took in these words, swallowed, and nodded, his gaze turning inward, almost
meditative, bemused, as with a measure of dignity he
stooped fatly to pick up his shirt, and his coat, where
they'd fallen to the floor, and as Momma and Daddy
watched united in silence he walked out the front
door not touching the door which stood open as if he
was through with touching anything in this house, this
bungalow he'd provided for Momma and me, ever
again. And then he was in his car, and we heard the
motor gunned a little too loud and then he was driving away, he was gone. And Momma and Daddy had
already forgotten him standing still wordless, looking
at each other. As if across a deep ravine they looked at
each other.

Till finally Momma said, "So you're not dead, after
all. I'd been wondering."

In the kitchen Momma bathed Daddy's wounded
face tenderly at the sink, then sat him in a chair, his
suede jacket removed, his shirt open and head back so
she could press ice cubes wrapped in towels against
his swelling eye. As the towels soaked with blood she
changed them. Her hands were trembling and she was
cursing under her breath *Oh God! oh Luke!* but she

remained calm, practical-fingered as a nurse. I helped her, breaking ice cubes out of the blue plastic trays from the refrigerator freezer so excited and eager I cracked each of them, they'd never be good again. Momma was saying, "Oh Luke, you let that man hit you, hit your face, oh God I was scared you'd kill him," and Daddy said shrugging, but you could see he was pleased with himself, "Chloe, I'm beyond that, now. I'm not like that now." Out of an inside pocket of his blood-splattered jacket he'd taken a handgun, and laid it on the kitchen table within easy reach. It was metallic-blue, dully gleaming, a revolver with a blunt snub nose.

We might have been waiting for the sound of a siren, for a sheriff's car to swing up to the curb. Quick purposeful footsteps up the front walk, onto the front porch. From time to time Momma would murmur she didn't think Maynard Zink would call the police, he wasn't the kind, it would reflect badly upon him, it would be Goddamned embarrassing for him, and Daddy said he hoped she was right, shrugging and laughing and wincing because his face was more cut up, battered, than he'd known, and maybe he was more wrung out, too, now the adrenaline rush had abated, his opponent was gone. I touched the gun with just my fingertips. So heavy, it didn't budge.

It was 11:30 P.M., and then midnight. Rain was blown against the windows, sometime it had started to rain and we hadn't noticed. Momma and Daddy were talking, and laughing, and their laughter was some-times a little wild. Momma looked young and excitable as a girl, a girl whose actions you couldn't predict any more than she could predict them herself. She'd fall to kissing Daddy and running her hands over him, his chest, his muscled shoulders, then leaning away when he tried to grab her wanting to kiss harder, as if I wasn't there. But it was all right I was there, so long past my bedtime, Daddy grinned at me and hugged me in the crook of his arm and called me his darling girl, his baby Ingrid he was so crazy for God knows he'd never leave again, did I forgive him?—did Momma forgive him? Momma said repeatedly, wiping her eyes, "Isn't this a surprise, Ingrid! Isn't this a revelation!"—the word "revelation" strange on her lips like some new, exotic word she'd just learned and was fascinated to utter. "The 'madman' has come back—for how long?" Daddy said, "Just long enough for you and Ingrid to pack. I've got plans."

Seemingly it was a secret between Daddy and me that we'd been together those five times without Momma knowing. And she would never know.

Not even years later not even then would I tell. If secrets don't bind together your life you have no life.

While Momma was tending to Daddy brisk and nurselike they'd begun drinking of course. Bottles of ale out of the refrigerator then Old Grand-Dad Kentucky straight bourbon whiskey taken down from a high kitchen shelf. Daddy smacked his lips. "So this is what you drink now, Chloe?" and Momma said sharply, "That's right. Now, with you."

The way then Daddy looked at Momma who was leaning against the sink regarding him with her hurt, impassioned eyes—Daddy with his angry-looking bruised eye and cut face, the smile draining from his lips—not even needing to touch each other. *If a man would ever look at me like that.*

I wanted to ask Daddy where we'd be going, would we be flying in one of the planes he'd taken us in years ago. I wanted to ask Daddy what it meant he was *wanted*, he was *in trouble* with the law. But the words choked in my throat. Daddy and Momma paid no attention to me, their eyes were only for each other.

I wanted to ask about Mr. Zink. *Piggy-Zink!* He'd looked so comical staggering out the door, his nose bloodied and the bald crown of his head flushed. Wouldn't we ever see him again? Would we have to leave this house? Mr. Zink was a nice man, he'd been nice to me. But—*Piggy-Zink!* You had to laugh.

Momma pressed ice cubes against Daddy's eye. What an ugly cut diagonal through Daddy's thick eyebrow, a sliver of flesh gouged out. He'd have a nasty scar, Momma said. One he couldn't hide.

Momma's mouth was pale now, bloodless-looking the bright lipstick rubbed off. Kissed off by Daddy. Her face showing the strain. And that way of talking, like walking on tiptoe, of someone who's been drinking, trying to shape each word. She said, "God damn it, Luke. Just showing up like this. No warning, my heart almost stopped! I didn't know if you were alive or dead, it's been—how long?—since you contacted me?"

Daddy said teasing, "Honey, if I was dead, wouldn't you know it? If I was gone forever from this world?"

Momma said, bitter, "There's been so many times I've thought that was so. Waking at night, from a dream of seeing you dead. It's like I gave you up, not once but lots of times. And I've been dead, too—but had to keep on living."

"Looks like you been doing all right. You're the kind of woman, somebody's going to take care of."

Momma laughed, and lifted her bourbon glass to her mouth. By this time too they were both smoking, out of Daddy's pack of Camels on the table. A book of matches, silver, stamped *Marita's*, no name familiar to me.

"This big-boy lover 'Maynard Zink'—who's he?" Daddy asked. When Momma wouldn't answer, pushing it, "He's—what? One of a kind, or—?" And still Momma wouldn't answer, wincing. "Or just one of a series? Huh?"

Momma whispered, "Fuck you."

Daddy laughed. "Hell, I'm a changed man now, Chloe. You saw, just now. I can go against my nature."

"It's late for that, Luke. Isn't it?"

Daddy spoke carefully as if it pained him to speak. He looked at me without seeing me, his words were all for her.

Saying, "I killed people in Nam, men, women, kids, Christ knows—water buffalo! But I never saw their faces. None of it was real to me. The more it happened, strafing, dropping napalm on 'em, poor fuckers, the more it wasn't real. And I wasn't real. I was stoned most of the time, or strung out. Heroin was just like tobacco, that common. It was like rations. I never worried my plane would be shot down, it was like cartoons in the movies. Once you're at a certain altitude. I knew I wouldn't die or if I did it didn't matter shit. A man *is* shit. So how can it matter?" Daddy was speaking earnestly now, looking at Momma who was sitting across the table from him, elbows on the table, hair disheveled half shielding her face and her gaze downcast like she was tired, so tired, all of us so tired, scared. "If I blew the head off a man who's upright walking talking stinking shit and everybody including his friends—including the cops—acknowledges that fact, you expect *me* to take it seriously? You expect *me* to go to Red Bank for it? Don't make me laugh. I'm shit in the eyes of God so anything I do or have done or will do isn't important."

Momma winced, saying, "You can't think that way, Luke. We've been over this. That's a wrong way of thinking."

"It's my way of thinking."

"You can change. I've changed."

"You? No you haven't. You're still my girl Chloe, and you'll always be my girl. Won't she, Ingrid?"— looking at me with a bright grin. "That doesn't change."

"I can go a day, a day and a night, without thinking of you. I've done it."

"Fuck you have. You haven't." Momma was shaking her head and Daddy said, raising his voice, "Any man you're with, anytime, ever—you're still my girl, and my wife. That won't change."

"I'm not a girl now. I'm old."

"You're not thirty years old."

"You ruined my life, and you ruined your own. That makes us both old."

"Like hell I ruined our lives," Daddy said, hurt. "I did what I had to do, I don't take shit from anybody. I don't regret it."

"Never mind about that. It makes me sick, I don't want to hear it."

"I'm a man of pride. I've got my pride."

"Yes, that's the trouble. That's always been the trouble."

"You saw me just now, with that asshole boyfriend—"

"He wasn't any 'boyfriend'—"

"—of yours. I could have hurt him bad, but I didn't. I went against my own nature, and I did it for you."

"Thanks!"

Daddy touched the butt of his gun, and the look in his face was regretful. "I let him hit me in the face," he said. "So you could see what I'm like now. How much I can take."

Momma shuddered. "Oh God, Luke. It hurt me, seeing that. It's a terrible thing to see someone you love get hurt. I was so scared you'd"—she paused, and glanced at me, her gaze going veiled—"do what you did that other time."

"Not in front of you and Ingrid. I wouldn't." Daddy took a large swallow of bourbon. Saying, laughing, so you couldn't tell if he was serious or not, "I can catch up with 'Maynard Zink' some other time."

These words, Momma didn't seem to hear.

Momma was looking at me like she just remembered me. Saying, in the careful-stepping way of a drunk, "Ingrid! Didn't I tell you to go to bed an hour ago?"

I said, "I'm not sleepy, Momma. I'm O.K."

"It's past one in the morning. Sweetie, you're exhausted, look at you."

Momma laid her dry warm palm against my forehead. Made that caressing-petting gesture I loved, I'd shut my eyes like a cat shuts its eyes being stroked, smoothing my hair back, drawing her hand down to the nape of my neck, and a little tickle there. I basked in Momma's touch, and in Daddy so close, seeing.

I said, whining, "I'm not, Momma. I'm wide awake like you."

They laughed at me, I must have been dazed with tiredness, and Daddy touched me, too, squeezing my arm, saying, "Put her to bed, Chloe. Then we can talk."

"*You* put her to bed."

"You're the mother."

"And thank God I am, since she hasn't got a father."

"She has. She knows she has. Don't you, Ingrid? That's why I'm here. I *am* her father."

Daddy reached for the matchbook and knocked it to the floor and I stooped to get it for him. *Marita's, Crystal Lake, Florida.*

A car passed in the street outside. We all listened.

Momma said bitterly, "We'd be expected to live like this? The three of us?"

"We'd live in Florida. I've got different places there I stay. It's a different world there."

Momma laughed. "Under what name, Luke? Or names? What would be our new names?"

Daddy shrugged. "There's different names I use, sure. It's been five years but I don't take any chances."

"Right. Look what happened to Vaughn."

"That's right. Look what happened to Vaughn."

"Do you know anything about that, Luke? Who killed him?"

Daddy looked at Momma lifting his hands and spreading the fingers wide in a gesture meant to signal not just innocence but bafflement. "No. No, I don't."

There was a pause. Then Momma weakened, that way she had so suddenly you never knew, it scared me to see her change even when I hated her. She said, begging, "Luke, please. I love you. It's right—I'll never love anyone else. But I can't listen to this. I don't even know what you're saying. My heart's racing like crazy, feel it?"—taking Daddy's hand and placing it against her chest and I could see the heartbeat in his hand.

Daddy leaned forward and kissed Momma on her pale hurt lips.

"We'll discuss it when we get there."

"Get where, Luke?"

"Where we're going. Tomorrow."

Momma began crying quietly. Her fingers to her eyes and the hot tears spilling through.

"We *are* going," Daddy said. "That's why I'm here. Right, baby?"

He was looking at me, and he was smiling. One side of his face swollen so he looked like a balloon wrongly inflated. Seeing Momma cry this time I was crying, too. So sleepy, my head swaying on my shoulders.

Daddy said, scolding, "Look at her. You're a bad influence, Chloe."

Surprising me then lifting me in his arms. So strong!—so tall! It was like I was a little girl again, lifted toward the ceiling, squealing as if I was being tickled but I was too sleepy, my arms and legs limp like dead weights. Momma was on her feet saying, "Luke, please—if you turned yourself in—" and Daddy said, amused, "Yeah?" and Momma said, "If you got a lawyer, Luke, in Port Oriskany—" and Daddy said, "Oh yeah? Tell me." Carrying me from the lighted kitchen to the back part of the house as Momma began to lose it shouting after us, "If you loved us, you would! If you loved us, you would!" Momma was drunk, and Daddy called back over his shoulder, the way you humor a drunk person, "You think I don't love you? Yeah?"

I remember: Daddy carrying me in his arms into the little room that was my own room separate from Momma's bringing me to my bed with the fawns and lambs painted on the headboard he'd never in his life set eyes upon but knew unerringly where it was, and now Momma was in the doorway crying, begging, "Jesus, Luke! If you loved us! You'd turn yourself in, or let us go." Daddy laid me on my bed and pulled the covers over me and stooped to kiss me on the cheek. Hot breathy whiskey-kiss, and his beard that scratched. Saying so soft Momma maybe couldn't hear, only me. "What've I got to do, to prove how much I love you? Blow us all away?"

But, in the morning, Daddy was gone.

In the night I'd been wakened by a telephone ringing and I'd heard voices but I was too groggy to get out of bed to investigate and in the morning suddenly I woke again hearing voices and I remembered the night before and I ran breathless out into the kitchen and there was Momma alone, hunched over at the table—Momma in her red lacy-rayon nightgown Mr. Zink had given her, her breasts hanging loose and heavy, the nipples showing through the thin fabric so I was stricken with shyness seeing her. Momma's eyes were reddened and puffy from crying, Momma had never looked so haggard. Her hair was matted like a crazy woman's on TV. She was barefoot, and even her feet looked knobby-boned, bluish-white, ugly. Momma sitting at the kitchen table that was still crowded with ale bottles and an ashtray overflowing with butts, Momma smoking a cigarette dropping ash on what I had to come closer to see was scattered bills?—money? The voices that had wakened me, bright and antic, were radio voices. It was 7:55 A.M.

I was scared and excited asking, "Where's Daddy?"

Momma squinted at me like the shape of me was hard to bring into focus. Like, swerving into her line of vision, her dreamy-hungover head, I was too much for her to absorb.

"Momma?—where's Daddy?"

I felt how empty the house was. Beneath the radio voices a terrible silence.

Momma's first response (she would deny afterward) was meant to be a joke—" 'Daddy'? There's no 'Daddy' here." Lips twitching in the vague quick smile of a woman in shock, eyes fixed on me shiny as glass.

I stared at her. Pulses beat in my eyes. If Momma'd taken up our twelve-inch carving knife and split her skull like a melon to show me the madness inside I could not have been more astonished.

"But—where's Daddy? What happened to Daddy?"

Still Momma kept up that smile, a smile turning hard. My eyes moved over the empty ale bottles, the empty Old Grand-Dad bottle and glasses in the sink, last night's supper dishes soaking. Blood-stiffened towels on the linoleum floor. Momma said jeering, "Must've dreamt it, silly. There's no 'Daddy' here, and never was. Not in *this* house."

Like walking in my sleep I went into the living room seeing the overturned furniture, the broken ceramic lamp that had been so beautiful, ugly mess of the night before. A white-faced skinny child in pajamas staring at herself in a crooked mirror. *Who's that? You have to laugh.*

I looked out the front window and there was no car

at the curb. I ran out sliding on ice on the front porch barefoot and shivering seeing only Momma's sexy little car she called it, a bronze Cougar Mr. Zink had helped her to buy, in the driveway. "Daddy? Daddy—?" I started to cry. Behind me Momma was yelling for me to shut the Goddamned door, get inside and shut the Goddamned door did I want everyone in the fucking neighborhood to know our private business?

Inside, I saw Momma coming at me and I ran down the hall into her bedroom—"Daddy! Daddy!"—but the room was empty, just the smell of him, a powerful smell of him that hit me like a blow, the hair oil, the sweaty man-smell. Sheets that looked like they'd been torn off the bed, a pillow on the floor like something thrown down in rage. Momma's clothes, the cute little black sweater, her jeans, black bra and panties on the floor. I ran to the window staring out seeing—what? A rotted fence at the rear of the property, tall thistles and grasses covered in dewy snow. During the night, the rain had frozen.

Momma followed me into the bedroom stumbling and scolding, slapping at me as I tried to duck under her hand. "Just shut your mouth!" she cried. "Nobody's here, and he never was here! What do you mean, mocking your mother?"

This went on for a while, I was crying and furious and Momma was in her crazy state, then Momma quieted down, that way she had of doing, like a wildfire burning itself out. Around 8:30 A.M. she called to me to come out from where I was hiding (I'd crawled under my bed), she was in the kitchen and back at the table her face washed now and a bathrobe over her night-gown, though she was still barefoot and her hair had not been combed. Except for the money and two glasses of fruit juice the table had been cleared. "Ingrid honey, come help me? Please?" Momma said. Sweet as sugar.

Explaining this: at 4:30 A.M. a call had come for my father from a friend of his warning him to get away from the house, and out of Tintern Falls as quickly as possible. Somebody had alerted the sheriff's office that Lucas Boone was back. So he'd left, he'd left without being able to say good-bye to me but he'd told Momma to tell me how much he loved me. He'd get in touch with us he'd promised. And in the meantime, there was this money he wanted us to have and Momma wanted my assistance now to count.

My eyes were sore from crying. I approached Momma with caution like a dog that's been kicked too many times. But seeing Momma was calm now—she *was* calm. Smiling like she loved her little girl, for sure she loved her little girl, would never let anyone hurt *her*.

And there was the orange juice bright as orange neon, a glass for Momma and a glass for Ingrid and I was famished with hunger.

Craziness does that, makes you famished. Blood sugar drops, you start hearing voices and seeing things, scurrying black bugs, sparks shooting off light-bulbs or people's eyes, weird-faced demons in shiny surfaces. Even in a kitchen, any shiny service. You learn quick to ingest any nourishment offered you from any source.

Loving any guy who'd shoot up with me, pressing the sweet sharp needle into my arm.

So I sat with Momma that morning. In the kitchen

of the little clapboard bungalow on North End Avenue, Tintern Falls. From which we'd have been evicted by the landlord like deadbeats if we hadn't been quick and prideful enough to move out ourselves, that very day. Momma used to say, You got to know when to move. More important than knowing when to stay put.

Sat with Momma and the two of us absorbed in counting our wealth of bills. Never seen anything like it before! Three times counting, because each time we'd get a different sum. And a fourth time, giddy and laughing like little girls together. Some of the bills fluttered to the floor out of Momma's hands, I was the one to retrieve them. Momma'd get dizzy leaning over too sharp. I never stopped to wonder why if Mr. Zink had called them, and who else would have called them?—the Eden County sheriff's men hadn't showed up at the house. Or why, warned they were coming like she'd said, Momma hadn't even put on her clothes. Not till years later realizing: Chloe Boone in the shrewdness of desperation must have arranged for that warning call to Lucas Boone herself. Must have slipped out of bed once my father was safely asleep and in stealth telephoned a mutual friend, some man with whom, who knows why, she was closer now than this man was with Lucas Boone. And told him in a low panicked voice her situation. *Help me! Help me! I'll make it up to you! please!* And this man for Momma's sake called the house shortly afterward rousing Daddy from bed, sounding the alarm. *Somebody's tipped off the sheriff. You better get the hell out.* And Daddy believed him for why shouldn't he have believed him, this man was Daddy's friend. Anyway it was a world of sudden arrivals and more sudden departures. A world of guns that might be fired, or might not. A world of sheriff's deputies surrounding the house while you slept, yelling *Open up! Open up!* Breaking down doors in the night.

So my father Lucas Boone threw on his clothes. Left money for his wife and little girl he was so crazy for he'd maybe have had to kill them to prove it. Left by night, drove away fast in his car rented under some stranger's name.

But knowing none of this at the time. Guessing none of this, that chilly-bright morning in November. Sitting excited and happy with Momma at the kitchen table drinking our orange juice and eating stale honey-glazed doughnuts sorting the money Daddy had left for us into piles the neatest we could make them with our sticky fingers: $20 bills, $50 bills, $100 bills! Momma kept marveling like a drunk woman Can you believe it, honey? *Can you believe it?*

There were eleven $100 bills there. Our final count was $4,860.

"Separated"

In Momma's bronze Cougar, pulling a yellow U-Haul trailer, we followed the Chautauqua River forty miles southeast, upriver to live in Mt. Ephraim in the next county, which was Chautauqua County. Within days Momma impressed the owner of Miss Flora Wells Fine Ladies' Clothes & Custom Tailoring she was not just sharp enough to clerk in the store but a skilled seamstress besides. Our "rental unit" was the second floor of a two-story woodframe house on Mohawk Street, a block uphill from the river. Momma said it was only temporary, we'd be moving to a better place soon. She spent our money from Daddy sparingly, fearful of putting it in any bank (*Wouldn't they know? wouldn't they ask: where did* you *get so much money?*) but she hid it in shrewd places, and always carried five of the $100 bills on her person. Momma was terrified of being really poor, dirt-poor, and men would know, always men can sniff out the degree of your desperation Momma believed, and force you to do things you don't want to do or don't exactly want to do at that time or in that place or in that way. When you have your own money, Momma said, you have power. But you can lose it Goddamned fast.

Momma made this vow many times sober and not-so-sober. She'd never open herself up to any man again in her life. Once was enough, and more than enough.

In Mt. Ephraim, which was a small city of about nineteen thousand people, nobody knew who we were. The name "Boone" seemed to be just a name. I started in a new school where there weren't any cousins to identify me. It was a happy time I think. I was eager to make friends and soon counted four or five girls as my close friends though Momma didn't think it was a good idea for me to invite them back to our apartment where many things remained in boxes and suitcases weeks after we'd moved in. Momma had no serious man friend in Mt. Ephraim and did not want one. But there was always male attention, and men. But never any man she guessed might be married. She always explained that she herself was married, though *separated*. Like *separated* was a disease so rare you might almost take pride in it.

Mr. Zink did not contact Momma, so far as I knew. Nor did Momma contact him, even to apologize. Sometimes, a drink in hand, in one of her moods, she would whisper, "My God!—did I really tell that poor man, that good decent trusting pathetic man, I was just there for the *money?*" And she'd shudder, and laugh, though she was disgusted, too. The more disgust you feel, you might as well laugh.

I said, gnawing at a thumbnail, "It's Daddy you should feel bad about."

Momma said, not looking at me, "Shut up about 'Daddy.' I've told you."

I danced out of reach of her swinging hand knowing that, at such a time, Momma would not make the effort to get up and chase me.

"Why? *Why* should I shut up?"

"Because 'Daddy' is gone."

"Gone where?"

"Gone."

"Florida?"

"I don't know. *Gone.*" Momma sighed, and shook her head, her hair she wore in a tight French twist for Miss Flora Wells but let fall loose as soon as she got home. "Honey, we've got to think about a divorce. I've got to think about a divorce. Putting my life in order. Some kind of . . . order. I'm going to be thirty-one years old." But her voice would trail off and her eyes lose their sharp focus like she was staring into some emptiness instead of at me.

Momma's liquor of choice was Old Grand-Dad now. Expensive, she admitted, but the quality is worth it.

Mohawk Street was paved for several blocks then turned abruptly to gravel and dirt, gravel and mud in wet weather. About a mile away, back another gravel road, there was a limestone quarry; an abandoned quarry where, kids in the neighborhood told me, a man's body was trapped in water thirty feet deep. Inside the cab of a truck he'd been driving. There had been an accident and the truck backed through a fence and sank into the water and they'd sent divers down but couldn't locate him. There were NO TRES-PASSING signs posted on the property but my new friends led me into the quarry which was a place so dug-up and scooped-out with strange steep hills of pebbled stone and abandoned vehicles and tools it looked like the landscape of another planet. Our voices echoed, shouting. We tossed rocks into the deep water where they sank with few ripples as if something was sucking them down.

If it was dusk, or a darkish day, we scared one another seeing the drowned man's ghost.

My first acid trip, years later, it was that *drowned man* I saw, out of so many things I might have!

There's a stark cold odor of stone I can smell right now. And that odor of deep, lightless water.

My new friends and classmates asked about my father sometimes. Did I have a father?—where was he? And my friends' mothers, curious, not meaning to be rude, or cruel. And I would smile and repeat what Momma instructed: I had a father, but he wasn't living with us right now. My father had been in the Vietnam War and was wounded. My father and mother are *separated*.

Sometimes I said, echoing Momma, *separated for the foreseeable future.*

And my friends' mothers did regard me with sympathy, I thought. Or maybe pity. Or distrust. Their eyes moving over me, weighing my words, calculating what this might mean; if it signaled some danger to them and their marriages. A woman who looked like Chloe Boone living alone with just her young daughter, no man. A woman who was supporting herself. A woman they knew nothing of except what rumors flew among them that might be reliable, or might not.

* * *

It was two months since we'd left Tintern Falls, then three. It was the New Year, Momma said. We had not yet unpacked all our things but we were settled in Mt. Ephraim, in the woodframe house on Mohawk Street, for the time being. Momma had her job at Flora Wells' and I counted five, six new friends, not just girls but boys, too. My hair was wavy as my mother's, and the same pale-blond color, and there were older boys who watched me, smiled and called me *Doll*. My blood leapt to see their eyes on me, and to know they were speaking of me to one another. In my own sharp, critical eyes I was not "pretty" nor even "cute" but it was the boys' eyes that mattered.

Walking across snow-stubbled fields near our house I would look up eagerly at the sound of a small airplane passing overhead. That whining-droning sound, unmistakable in the distance, gradually increasing in volume until it seemed deafening. Sometimes the shadow of a low-flying plane would glide rapidly across the earth and slice through me like a blade!—and I would stand frozen, transfixed, staring after the plane until it grew smaller and smaller and disappeared into the distance.

Then one day, this day I am thinking of, a winter day, in late winter, maybe March. A sky glaring like tin and frost patterns on our apartment windows and when Momma came home from the dress shop she switched on the lights seeing me in the kitchen, at the kitchen table, and there was the envelope addressed to MRS. CHLOE BOONE at our Mohawk Street, Mt. Ephraim address lying on the table. The envelope had been opened but its contents were pushed back inside.

Momma's eyes leapt like a cat's. Her lips shaped some little cry or plea—"Oh God."

Momma always opened mail with a pleased anxious look, a frown between her eyebrows. Now she picked up this envelope with the handwriting she knew, would have recognized from the doorway five feet away in the instant she switched on the light, and that same frown appeared fleetingly, before she took the Polaroids out of the envelope, and saw. And her mouth dropped open, and the blood drained from her face. She uttered a wail like somebody had struck her in the belly.

There were three snapshots, three perspectives.

Three views of Maynard Zink.

In the first, the dead man, the side of his face so shiny and glutinous with blood he's unrecognizable, is seen from his right side, lying on his back; his stomach protrudes above his belt but looks soft, flaccid, part-collapsed under its own weight. The fleshy face is turned away from the camera as if in shame of what has happened to him, what he's become.

In the second, the dead man, now clearly Maynard Zink, is seen from his left side, at a closer range, so the ravaged front of his face, the eyes, are exposed. Dead eyes, the color and texture of peeled grapes. The nose is bulbous, the mask of blood cruelly comic like an ill-fitting Halloween mask. There appears to be a bullet hole in the throat, gleaming with blood. Both the man's arms are outflung as if in protest.

In the third, the starkest shot, the dead man is seen from directly overhead. The camera is being held above him at a distance of about three feet, the invisible photographer standing at the dead man's feet. The dead man might almost be standing erect against a weirdly carpeted, bloodied wall—it takes a second to see, no, he's lying on his back, on a floor. He's *down*. He's *dead*. The large, somber head is turned fatly to its left, the chins creased. The sightless eyes are cast sidelong, the mustache beaded with blood, the slack lips parted. There are crude gashes, bullet holes, in the man's chest, in his shirt with its smart blue stripes, and again the bloody hole in his throat, exposing something white. Even the thinning strands of hair he has so carefully combed to disguise his balding crown have been rudely displaced, as if in a prank. There are table legs, or desk legs, a few inches behind the dead man's head, and the edge of a carpet soaked in blood.

Momma was whispering, "Oh God oh God oh God." Stumbling dazed to sit down in one of the dinette chairs, reaching out blindly for my hand, my hand that eluded her at first, groping for my hand and squeezing the fingers like she wanted to break them. My fingers were limp, cold and unresponsive. There was no strength in them. I had nothing to say. My throat was shut tight. Momma continued examining the Polaroids as if they might be something else if she looked at them the right way. They were so brightly colored, seeing them upside down from a short distance you thought they must be of something festive like a Christmas tree, a flower bed. Momma whispered to herself now breathing hard, quick short hard breaths, and after a while she got to her feet, went to the sink and tore up the Polaroids quickly into small pieces and burned them with her lighter and washed the ashes down the drain, running the water from both faucets hard and loud. Not looking at me, and I did not look at her. Then coming stumbling to where I was sitting, had been sitting unmoving for almost two hours, stooping over me clumsy and sobbing and her hot damp breath in my neck, hugging me, gripping me tight, "You never saw anything, Ingrid. You never saw anything. *You never saw anything.*"

Two Clocks

He said, for a pilot there are just two times basically.

The time on the ground, and the time in the air.

The one clock is slower than the other. Like the two times in your life: when something happens, and when it doesn't.

When you're in the air and the clock really speeds up everything goes white, roaring, collapsed, blind. One day, a plane will be your coffin. That's a probable fact. It's a fact you learn to live with.

Those times he'd almost crashed but didn't, exactly. In Vietnam and a few times back home. Climbed out of the plane and standing on solid ground again he discovered he'd become older, in the air.

The clock goes on, you have to catch up.

The Joker

Ever after that, it was our secret between us, Momma's and mine. You'd think it would draw us closer, but no. That was the wedge splitting us apart.

Lots of things, I've forgotten. Every drug you take, every sweet-swooning moment it's the way into oblivion.

A guy I knew once, saying if all AMERICA swallowed enough LSD at a single moment all our history would be erased.

When I was a junkie even before I was Dog-girl I loved that door that swings open and you're walking toward it faster and faster and on the other side— nothing. For sure, you're going to step through. You're saved.

Never got around to believing Jesus Christ is my savior, or anything to do with God, much. If you start taking drugs even just grass, grass I began smoking in high school I mean when I was high school age going out with older guys from Port Oriskany, then the harder kind, the kind people die for, you start that young you bypass any craving for God.

Lots of things, you forget. Like my father said it's shit. Once you get to a certain altitude. Shit in the eyes of God whether there even *is* God.

So I don't remember how I know this. Whether Momma actually told me, or I found out some other way. Hard to think Momma would be the one to tell because we never talked about it afterward. We might allude to "when *it* happened," "when *that* happened," the way you do in a family or living with anybody you work up some kind of shorthand for not-saying what you need to say but can't. Anyway I knew that Maynard Zink had been killed, shot dead in Zink's Real Estate & Home Insurance on Main Street, Tintern Falls, his wallet emptied of cash and credit cards and a small safe emptied of an estimated $6,000 so police believed it was robbery, the primary motive was robbery. When Mr. Zink hadn't returned home on a weekday evening by 7 P.M. and hadn't answered his wife's calls she drove downtown to the office, found the rear door unlocked and Mr. Zink inside. He was lying on his back, shot at close range in the heart, the chest, the throat with a .38 caliber pistol. He was lying on a blood-soaked carpet by the opened safe and his desk where amid many papers and documents his wallet had been tossed. Police theorized that the killer or killers had forced their way inside after the office was closed, everyone gone home but Maynard Zink, and they'd forced him to unlock his safe and then shot him, point-blank. No one reported hearing gunshots, and no witnesses came forward. No fingerprints other than Mr. Zink's and his employees' were found at the crime scene. The murder weapon was never found. It was said that Maynard Zink was much loved in Tintern Falls, which was the city of his birth. He had no known enemies, he was a popular president of the local Chamber of Commerce and a deacon in the Lutheran church and a past officer of the local Parent-Teacher Association. Forty-nine years old when he died.

The killer or killers would never be identified. Men with police records in the area were questioned, but the investigation came to nothing. The credit cards never turned up.

It's almost fifteen years later, the case must still be open.

After the Polaroids, Momma began drinking heavily. There was the time before, and there was the time after. The clock goes on, you're older. You have to catch up.

This is what I hear: Momma's voice that's her new drunk-marveling voice, over the phone to one of her man friends who's always calling her or they wake me up having a nightcap in the kitchen at 3 A.M. after he's brought her home from wherever they've been, "Say, you know?—God is the joker in the deck. God's the fucking joker, y'know?"—Momma making this declaration, laughing like it's some new, fresh discovery she's just made that day, can't wait to share such wisdom, "You never know what He's going to do next, but you know He's going to do something. The *joker!*"

Easy Lay

Hard to believe how *popular* I was. At Mt. Ephraim High School where I was in ninth grade that spring. Counted *ten*, *twelve*, *sixteen*, *nineteen* new friends! Not just boys in my class but popular juniors and seniors, athletes began to notice me, smiled and called me *Doll*, *Doll-girl*, *Ingrid*, *In-grie*. Word spreads fast, who the good-looking ninth-grade girls are. Asked me on dates, but Momma wouldn't allow it saying I was too young. Tried to get my phone number to call. Whispering, staring. A guy named Dean in jeans, T-shirt, biker boots running his thumb along the row of ninth-grade lockers prowling the ninth-grade corridor to check *Doll-girl* out. But it was the popular boys, a better class of boys I sought. I loved it, their attention! That feeling leaves you sick and faint with excitement knowing you're *popular!* Couldn't get enough of it drifting through school corridors between classes as in a dream smiling Hello! hi! *hi there!* imitating the pretty popular older girls because in truth I had no friends, a horse-faced girl named Bernice who talked about me behind my back saying I had bedbugs, a boy named Jig from Mohawk Street who talked me into kissing him openmouthed then laughed at me when I started to choke and gag and somebody told me he'd written something nasty about INGRID BOONE in all the boys' lavatories at school. But I had certain friends I listed their names in code in my notebook with a ☆ by the special ones and there was a special-special list of boys all ♡ ♡ ♡ ♡. And there was a special list growing longer with each passing day of boys and girls who had insulted me, cut me to the heart, these were marked ☠ the way the mystery-detective novels were marked at the public library, on their peeling spines. Marked for Death. But truly I *was* pretty, and I *was* popular. Girls in my neighborhood were jealous of me the way their mothers were jealous of my mother with her blond hair, her face and figure and clothes and bronze Cougar. The clothes *I* wore, funky little tops and poor-boy sweaters and jeans snug in the rear, now I refused to wear most of what Momma sewed for me, made me look older than I was whatever age I was. And I'd started to smoke, carried my own cigarettes and a gilt-lettered matchbook from the Yewville Park Lane Hotel where one of Momma's man friends with money to spend took her certain weekends. And I was smart. My mind rattled on fast as a machine sometimes, ran its own way without my participation. So I'd know the answer to an algebra problem but not the steps to that answer. Or what a poem like Robert Frost's "The Road Not Taken" meant but not how to explain it. Stammering and going beet-red if called upon. Even by my English teacher Miss Elsworth who liked me. And the other teachers who were hopeful of me at first then grew impatient, exasperated. My problem was nerves I guess. Too nervous and excited to do well on tests

unless I memorized every possible question beforehand and wrote them out and even sometimes if I
made this exhausting effort it did no good, my blood
beat too hard, my thoughts ran wild. *You're stupid.
You're a bad girl. White trash. Going to hell like every
other Boone.* This voice I'd never heard in my life and
it was not a voice I acknowledged but at such times
taking tests and exams it rang unimpeded in my
head like a radio you can't shut off. But I excelled
in take-home assignments and homework in general
so a teacher like my social studies teacher Mrs. Hor-
nell would think I was cheating getting help from an
older student or a parent and if interrogated about
this I stammered and blushed and stared at the floor
scarcely able to whisper *No.* When I did my homework
my grades were A's except if I lost my homework to
some guy grabbing my duffel bag, turning it upside
down over the oil-splotched pavement behind the
high school teasing me calling me *Doll-girl* the way
they did. Or maybe I'd done the wrong questions in
the textbook, hadn't been listening when the teacher
gave the assignment. Or I was listening but staring so
hard at this guy Foxy sitting sprawled in his desk by
the window at the far side of the classroom ignoring
me, stared and stared at Foxy who'd hurt me and
never apologized so I didn't hear the teacher's dron-
ing voice. Or it was one of my feverish days scribbling
poems in my notebook! Poems about love, and dying,
and flying high above the earth, and white horses with
long streaming manes wild in the mountains. Cas-
cades of words filling up pages in my notebook like
the churning channels of water of Tintern Falls you
can stare at until you're hypnotized but you can never

determine their pattern except to know there *is* a pattern inside the falls. Or maybe I wasn't writing poems at all, maybe I was scribbling love letters to Foxy who had kissed me and run his hands over me and said he was crazy for me then hurt me squeezing my breast, turned mean when I told him stop and pinched my left nipple so I burst into tears, and he never apologized. Not a one of them ever apologized! Or letters to Dale, or Bibi, or Dorie, or Rich, or Carrie Kimble the "captain" of the varsity cheerleaders' "squad"—the senior girl I would have traded my soul, of all the girls of Mt. Ephraim High, to *be*. Or letters to Mr. Quincy our algebra teacher I wanted so desperately to please. Homely frog-face with his mean little bored half-smile, leaning his chin on his hand every day and his eyes trailing over most of his students in pity and contempt but I loved Mr. Quincy, I was terrorized by him, a clammy sweat broke out over me and my brain shuddered to a stop when he announced with his mocking smile *Spot quiz! Take out a clean sheet of paper and put away your books!* From Ingrid Boone a paper with so many corrections and X'd out problems it was virtually unreadable and no surprise when the quiz came back marked F- in red felt-tip pen. And once that shameful sheet of paper returned to me with the usual F- but also that time a swirling indignant question mark through my scrawled INGRID BONE—I had misspelled my own name! And Mr. Quincy staring at me hunched and thumbnail-biting in my seat like I was white trash as hopeless as Bernice Urken. Or I might be writing to Miss Elsworth my English teacher who was the only teacher who liked me though the fact that she liked me lessened her in my eyes. Or I might be writing to "Bunny" Heinz the boys' gym coach who ran my afternoon study hall like a drill sergeant on TV, wisecracking and harsh and unpredictable in his moods. Or I might be writing to the principal Mr. Cantry who led us in the Pledge of Allegiance at Friday assemblies with a high ringing sincere voice pressing his right hand against his fattish torso like an upright hog in that way scaring me *It's Mr. Zink!*—he had shaved his mustache and dyed his hair a tarnished-gray color but it lay in the same thin strands across his big head. If I'd swallowed a diet pill or two given to me by my friend Bonnie this vision was particularly convincing. It was not far-fetched, was it—Maynard Zink was the type of man to do such a thing, change his name and his profession, or maybe it was a trick to catch his murderer. Or a prank. A *second life*—one of those careers middle-aged men take up after the first halves of their lives are over. But in fact I never thought of Mr. Zink. Especially not the ugly-comical fat blood-splattered corpse somebody had made him into. Him on his back on a floor, arms outspread like he's crying *Why?* Anybody who asks a question that is not answered is a fool. You don't want to look at him, or acknowledge him. Never think of it. The evidence torn into pieces, a match set to them, and washed down the kitchen sink. Any more than I would think of the most disgusting things *maggots*, *guts*, *a guy coming in my mouth*, *pubic lice*. Ugh! Nor did I think of my father who was no longer Daddy but had no name. I was not even certain I remembered what he looked like, such a long time had passed. But if there's a chain-link fence I'll stare at it my skin prickling thinking *Somebody will slip through, you can't keep him out.* Momma never spoke of any of it, of course. Her fingers had been shaking like the worst kind of hangover setting fire to the Polaroid strips but she'd burnt them all, every last one. She'd vomited afterward into the toilet but that was the last of it. But sometimes she was afraid to answer the phone when it rang, rang, rang late at night. Though we had an unlisted number here in Mt. Ephraim and Momma hoped to be known as "Chloe McDiarmid." Yet sometimes not asleep though not fully awake I opened my eyes and saw Mr. Zink on his back trying to rise, blood bubbling out of a hole in his throat. But rapidly retreating like a sight fleetingly glimpsed through a telescope. If such a sight retreats in time as in space it is hopeless to try to retain it. I did wear the warm glen-plaid wool jacket and the sheepskin-lined boots Momma had purchased for me with money provided by Mr. Zink the previous Christmas and these were among my proudest possessions for the jacket was similar to a jacket worn by a pretty red-haired JV cheerleader Gail Ellen Ryan and the boots were similar to boots worn by Carrie Kimble. But that Christmas back in Tintern Falls was a long time ago, I'd been a child then and you can come almost to doubt that you were ever anyone other than who you are at the present time. Momma insisted that she'd made these purchases right here in Mt. Ephraim at the Hitching Post where after school I browsed sometimes with my friends Sandy and Bonnie giggling trying on clothes in the dressing rooms working up our courage to steal (you'd put on layers of clothes under your own) but the bitchy salesgirls had our number spying on us so we'd stroll over to Bar-B-Q Diner where we'd meet

guys from school, not ninth graders but older guys
sliding into our booth like we'd invited them grinning
at us especially me *Hi there, Ingrid! Got room for me,
In-grie?* Some jokes about my name and about BOONE
but I didn't know what they were, and gave no sign.
Things said of me or scrawled on walls but how would
I know what, and why care. And we'd smoke our cigarettes, drink Cokes fizzing with caffeine till my head
buzzed and we'd laugh, laugh like hyenas. Bonnie's
older sister's diet pills, prescription pills Bonnie stole
just a few at a time, plus the caffeine: WOW! Talking
screwing around with these cool guys, couldn't break
away, why lots of nights I didn't do my homework or if
I'd already done it in study hall it was taken from me
for somebody else's use. Or just taken, ripped or
tossed away. Funny! And if the guys wanted to go to
the movies at the mall, a show starting at 5:15 P.M. getting out at 7:30 P.M. And in the dark back rows where
the seats creaked when a guy you didn't know slipped
his arm around your shoulders and began to kiss you
forcing your head back like he wanted to snap your
neck forcing your mouth open so there was the terror
of choking on his tongue alive and thrusting like an
eel, and his sudden fingers between your legs, poking,
pinching, and if you began to choke, or clawed at his
hand, or thrashed your head from side to side panicked trying to escape he would lean back panting in
his seat whispering *Shit!* then get up and walk away.
Or if a guy had a car or his daddy's pickup and asked
to drive you home. And you knew it was an asshole
thing to do but you said *Sure!* Beer cans opened in
the parking lot, warm beer in dribbles down your
chin. A single can and you're dizzy, two cans and

you're what the guys call *smashed*. That tone of admiration and approval like Momma's drunk-marveling voice: *smashed*. And there was the old quarry road off Mohawk, bumpy treacherous with icy slush and low overhanging tree limbs heavy with snow and you squealed with laughter the car bounced so, bounced and rattled on its high tires, and already it was dark, it was night and no stars and the car's lurching headlights and you'd just gotten out of school, you'd been expected to drop by Flora Wells' to meet up with your mother for some purpose long forgotten. *Oh oh oh!*— waiting to see if he would drive the clumsy car too far, skid out onto the quarry ice and the ice would shatter beneath the weight of the car and you would all sink, drown a hideous death in freezing water. That trucker behind his windshield gazing up, a pilot behind his windshield gazing up, grinning, waiting. *Doll-girl, do me, huh? You know how? Don't play dumb.* How they would go from moaning how beautiful you are, how crazy they are for you to that sound of reproach and threat, it was always a surprise. But the kissing was so sweet, even the openmouthed kissing so sweet sometimes, and a guy's strong hands cradling your head, stroking your hair, gazing at you close-up like a lover on TV or in the movies like you *exist*, you *are there*. But sometimes the hands were hurtful, and the guy too drunk and you're not smashed enough not to be scared, and running stumbling sobbing and puking beer across a snowy debris-littered field to the rear of a neighbor's house and so through to Mohawk Street and back home where Momma was not waiting anyway. And next morning Momma bleary-eyed and pissed examining the glen-plaid jacket, sniffing the beer-vomit you've tried to wash out. *Ingrid?—what the hell are you up to?* But by then the panic was not only gone but forgotten. The swimming eyes and bruised mouth. Kept a scrupulous record of boys I "dated" but it wasn't always clear if these episodes had happened yet or were meant to happen someday soon. But if it had happened it *had happened* and was over with. And I wouldn't need to remember, or would confuse it with another time or something on TV or in a movie. Because I *was* smart: reasoning I couldn't be pregnant, the stuff that came out of him I knew to call sperm hadn't gone *in*. Just dribbled on my thighs, in my pubic fuzz. Where I'd touched it afterward examining it on my finger, just—nothing. Clear wetness a little sticky, and no smell. Like a more transparent snot. But not nasty like snot. Reasoning too I was too skinny, tiny breasts and my pelvic bones jutting, I was thirteen years old and hadn't begun "my periods" yet, one of the last girls in ninth grade according to the girls' gym teacher who kept a weird record of such things. And how strange to me that my face was so different to the outer eye than I knew it to be from inside. My fevered skin, that itched and demanded scratching. I would stare in amazement at my reflection in any mirrored surface—*Is that me?— Ingrid?* It was a sort of a joke. Unless it was a trick. But who was playing the trick? The girls' lavatory bluish-foul with smoke though smoking was forbidden so I would lean close to the mirror in wonder as if to kiss the staring blond girl with the wide-set brown eyes lightly threaded with veins but the skin actually clear-looking. *My God am I pretty?—how is it possible I am pretty?* Discovering then a tiny red pimple beside my mouth, a budding dull-red lump at my hairline, *C'n I borrow a cigarette, Ingrid?* a girl would ask and my heart would swell in pride. *Sure! Take two.* How proud I was counting *five, six, nine, eleven* girlfriends. And more boys asking me out, or following me home. But were these girls I could trust?—what were they saying behind my back? Their eyes narrowing when I passed by them in the cafeteria, smirking when Miss Elsworth read my essay "Winter Riverscape" to the class, a conspicuous red A+ beside my name. That was the cruel secret of friendships at Mt. Ephraim High I was beginning to learn. But I would never give up. Each morning vowing to make a new friend, or anyway to try. Could be a girl or a boy, in ninth grade, or tenth, or eleventh, or most prized of all a senior. Because in fact I had no friends, not a single girl not even Bernice. Not a single boy who would not betray me. But I forced myself to smile like Carrie Kimble *H'lo Dale! Hi Dorie! Hi Foxy!* moving in the noontime crush jostled along the corridor to the cafeteria my eyes stark and staring as a zombie's. And later in the day taking a certain stairs hurrying from one end of the hall to the other where Kirk Belknap who was a senior dark-haired and good-looking a basketball player with a terrific smile left his biology class to go downstairs to his sixth-period class which was gym and by chance I would be headed downstairs too beside him, or as close to beside him as possible *Hi Kirk!* and if he was talking and laughing with his friends he might not hear so I would say a little louder *HI KIRK!* and he would glance back at me quizzical and possibly a little annoyed not recognizing me or not remembering my name but mumbling *Yeah, hi*

reddening as one of his buddies poked him in the ribs
and the guys moved on together eyeing *Doll-girl* in
that way that scared and excited me like somebody
bringing a lighted match up close to my hair: WOW!
And one afternoon after school there was Kirk in his
car cruising the curb where I was walking by myself
and he leaned out his window asking in the nicest
voice how'd I like a ride home? and I could not believe
my eyes who it was, I must have stared amazed and
there was a beat or two before I managed to say
Sure!—thanks! and lots of people were watching, girls
stricken with envy, and we rode around talking and
smoking cigarettes and listening to the radio and Kirk
told me all sorts of things about himself I would never
have guessed such as he wanted to be a doctor minis-
tering unto the poor someday, possibly in the Peace
Corps, and he had three basketball scholarships
offered him by colleges but couldn't make up his mind
which one to accept, and he'd had bad luck with girls,
in his opinion at least, there was always some hurt
feelings and misunderstandings and he was damned if
he caught on why. Driving in sleety rain north of Mt.
Ephraim and along the river following the railroad
tracks the way I remembered from some other time
unless it was a dream I was remembering, so sweet.
And we stopped at a place that sold fishermen's supplies plus beer and liquor and the owner seemed to
know Kirk so sold him two six-packs of ale though he
was underage, this strong dark ale like nothing I had
ever tasted before Kirk said takes getting used to. And
in a hidden place we parked above the river and drank
and talked and laughed listening to the radio and I
was snuggled in Kirk's arms like I'd been there many

times, so peaceful, and we were kissing and it was
gentle like no other kissing of my life but like kissing
on TV or in the movies and Kirk was saying over and
over like the lyrics of a song *Ingrid you're so pretty!*
Ingrid you're so special! and he groaned he was so
crazy for me, wanted me so, and it was a long time
later I tried to wake up pushing his hands away where
he was inside my clothes and he'd opened his trousers
like some of the guys want to but Kirk was gentle,
saying *Ingrid?—let's go in the backseat O.K.?* and I
saw how big his penis was, big for *me*, I was proud
how big it was for *me*, and I was sleepy and sort of
sickish saying *Gee I don't know, maybe I should go*
back home? and Kirk said *But honey I love you, I'm*
crazy about you and I said in this slow dazed voice
Gee I don't know, I guess not but he wasn't listening,
pushing against me, and running his hands over me,
and we never needed to go into the backseat.

Gorgeous

Counted eleven bites on myself. Mosquitoes? Ticks? Bedbugs? On my feet, ankles, calves, thighs. Stomach, midriff where my ribs stretched my tight skin. One on the underside of my tiny left breast. There was a fascination in it: some were angry new swellings I'd made bleed with my nails, miserable from the itching. Others were older bites that had begun to heal I'd roused into itching again with my roving nails. Sometimes my entire lower body throbbed with itching especially at night when I couldn't sleep my heart beating too fast and it was like my skin had gone crazy and was turned mutinous against itself and I'd bite my lip hard holding off as long as I could until tears spilled from my eyes and I couldn't bear it one more second and in a luxury of abandon sobbing with relief I would rake my nails hard hard HARD against the bleeding bumps and welts.

Oh God oh God oh.

There were certain things written about INGRID BOONE in the boys' lavatories at Mt. Ephraim High School. And maybe on outside walls, I didn't know. I didn't look, and I didn't know. My boyfriends were a shifting lot. A guy crazy about me one night might not

seem to notice me when I walked into the school cafeteria next day. I had close girlfriends but they talked
about me behind my back. I knew but I didn't know in
such a way that *they* knew—that had to be the basis of
my friendships. And with guys, too. There has to be
some basis. You can't trust them but you don't want
them to know because then they won't like you at all.
One of the men teachers must've seen something ugly
on a wall and I was called one day to the infirmary
where the school nurse asked me in this sort of
embarrassed voice did I have anything to ask her? any
questions of a *personal-medical* nature? I did, I had
plenty of questions but not to ask *her*. So I sat there
staring at the floor my face gone hot. Scratched at
something itchy on the inside of my elbow till I drew
blood.

I was fifteen years old now, and in tenth grade at
the high school. I was small for my age, lanky-armed
and -legged, hadn't begun my periods yet which
would've made me a freak if anybody knew but I kept
that secret for sure.

I felt very mature to myself. No matter how I
looked. Calling my mother MOTHER now and not
MOMMA. I hated that baby name!

Thinking of MOMMA, I mean MOTHER. And my
nails start roaming.

Weird: scratching an old almost-healed bite or sore
my nails would discover a new one, I'd swear it hadn't
been there a minute before. Strange-shaped striated
rashes or swellings, maybe a pimple, a hive caused by
some mysterious allergy. Fewer bites on my face
which was damned lucky. But overnight there might
appear a string of nasty hard pimples at my hairline,

itching and throbbing like hell. Mysterious bites, bumps on my scalp. Once, a bump the size of a robin's egg—Momma, I mean Mother, decided it had to be a spider bite. Those tiny poison ivy pustules sprouting between my fingers I'd SCRATCH SCRATCH SCRATCH till they burst and a runny liquid leaked from them but the itching only got worse. Scratch off my skin in patches but the itching only got worse.

Terrible itching-throbbing inside my right ear once in grade school I was almost crazy with it desperate poking a sharp pencil inside my ear and the teacher grabbed my hand and took me to the school nurse and she said My God you've got poison ivy inside your ear. I'd spread the hard little pustules from my ankles to my ear, on my nails.

This woman I was learning to call Mother stared at me sometimes appalled, disgusted or guilty-acting—so many *insect bites*, obviously our apartment wasn't clean. *What kind of a housekeeper is Chloe Boone?* It was true we'd inherited an infestation of roaches in our four-room upstairs apartment at 119 Mohawk Street and there was an inexhaustible supply of ants of various sizes rising through the floorboards or marching along exposed pipes or tracking across the kitchen ceiling to drop, like exclamation points, in somebody's plate. You could spray, and spray, and spray until you were sick to your stomach but it wouldn't help, much. There were spiders coming into the house as the weather cooled, and a spider bite *hurts*. In warm weather there were mosquitoes. And there were ticks which were the nastiest the most indestructible of all insects, you had to dig a tick out of your flesh with a sterilized pin and if part of the tick broke off and was left inside the bite would become infected and you'd have a fever, nausea. And such wild itching. And there were bedbugs once, to Mother's shame though she would never admit to it, the one thing you never admitted to was bedbugs, or some even worse thing *pubic lice* I'd heard whispered of and it made me sick to imagine.

Pubic?—lice?

Never mind, Mother said.

One day soon I would learn what *pubic lice* was. But not just yet.

My boyfriends were kept secret from Mother out of spite not wanting her to know *Guys love me too—not just you.* I counted so many listing them in my notebook ♡ ♡ ♡ then X'ing them out when we broke up which was sometimes only a few days after we'd begun going together. None of it had much to do with me, but I kept a scrupulous record.

Mother was hurt I never wore the clothes she sewed for me now. Never wore dresses, skirts—nobody did. Sweaters, jeans, jackets, boots. A few of the guys gave me money, older guys not in school I'd meet downtown and I'd buy clothes, funky hip-hugger belts, once a Timex watch with a good-looking leather band. Mother saw, and asked where'd that come from and I said what? where did what come from? and slammed out of the apartment. Went to make a telephone call, I didn't have to take any shit from *her*.

MOTHER I was calling her not MOMMA though sometimes I'd slip and say MOMMA and she'd pretend not to notice though I knew she'd be smiling, that was the kind of thing made her smile. Much of the time

MOTHER was strange on my lips like I'd been shot with novocaine. And strange to my mother's ears, hurtful, like some kind of secret insult. She'd beg me for God's sake Ingrid stop *scratching*, what are you doing to yourself? Do you want to scar your face?

Tried to forbid me but even in her watchful presence I could rake my nails lovingly in secret across my serrated skin, draw pinpoints of blood and take a spiteful pleasure in it. I never thought of scarring, of permanent injury like some faces you see pocked with acne scars, I thought only of SCRATCHING.

During summers which were so hot, humid, airless the insect bites were worse of course. Driving out with guys, and parking in their cars or pickups, or out on the ground, that's where you pick up ticks. But the mosquitoes were everywhere, even with our screened windows. Sometimes in fascination I'd count twenty, twenty-five, even thirty insect bites, from between my toes to my scalp, the very act of counting these bites repulsive to Mother. (Who had her own bites, not so many but enough. She'd douse them with stinging Noxzema the smell of which made me sickish.) A certain kind of beer made me break out in hives within minutes plus chocolate, citrus fruits, potato chips and cola drinks, coffee too it was said because of the caffeine, but I avoided none of these, I took a morbid interest in experimenting: how many minutes after I ate a candy bar would the first itchy red bump appear. Or maybe it was nerves. One of Mother's man friends Mr. Dilts of Dilts Hardware said of me that I was *nerved-up* like a young filly. His eyes narrowed to winking and his tongue moist in the corner of his mouth.

No one hated and feared doctors more than my mother. It had been a Yewville doctor, she always said, who'd let her baby boy die of meningitis he hadn't treated quick enough, the baby had died of medical neglect because the baby's parents hadn't had hospital insurance, yet Mother insisted upon taking me to a doctor in Mt. Ephraim to examine my bites, rashes, lumps, pimples, hives, but that day my skin wasn't too bad, the doctor diagnosed just normal adolescent-type skin plus a few insect bites like everybody has more or less, what's the problem? Charged us $35 for a five-minute examination and made out a prescription for a few ounces of a greasy ointment in a tube, had less effect than Noxzema and cost ten times as much.

I refused to get in the car with Mother, to drive home. I said, "If you weren't always watching me, *Mother*, my fucking skin wouldn't *itch*."

In fact, Mother wasn't watching me at all, she had her own life I didn't give a shit for. I had my own friends, and lots of friends, and even if I didn't I had my poetry I wrote showing only to my English teacher who praised me, Miss Elsworth was my only friend you might say. Because how could I trust anybody else.

Mother was putting more and more emphasis on how she looked, now she was getting older, and *older* began to show. Still she was good-looking, and knew how to dress. *Gorgeous* was a favorite word of hers she used a lot in conversation, one of her man friends greeted her with it *Hi Gorgeous!* I'd overhear, and roll my eyes. Still, Mother looked O.K. In Flora Wells' shop where I'd spy on her sometimes when walking past she had the look of a stranger who belonged in that plush-rose interior, her hair in a French twist and nails lacquered and face a perfect cosmetic mask she layered on thick in the morning and "freshened up" during the day. Mother was an expert at disguising blemishes on her own skin, her skin that was sensitive too, erasing as if by magic dark circles beneath her eyes. She wore Revlon lipsticks, deep earthy-crimson colors, plum-bronze, sometimes a frosty melon-pink of the color Mt. Ephraim cheerleaders wore. Plus eyeliner, mascara, smoky-blue eye shadow to make her eyes enormous. There were painkiller pills she got from a friend to help her through hangover mornings, and these made her eyes moist, dreamy. At the dress shop Mother was always the lady, for sure! Wearing the very kinds of expensive clothes Flora Wells sold her customers. Other times, weekends especially, Mother wore bright lipstick, her hair loose on her shoulders and frizzed until it seemed to float about her head, snug-fitting velvet pants, miniskirts or -dresses, white leather disco boots, sexy earrings. Saying it didn't matter if the man you're with is nobody you much care for, other men will be looking you over, too. It's the other men, the men you haven't yet met, one of them who'll maybe change your life, you're fixing yourself up for.

Why I came to have such quarrels with my mother, to hate and wish dead my mother, I don't know. There was hardly anything she ever told me didn't turn out to be true.

That day I counted eleven bites on myself was the day I was scheduled to read a poem at the awards assembly at the high school, I knew it was a terrible mistake to agree to read a poem, any poem but especially a poem by Ingrid Boone everyone would sneer at, and maybe they would laugh at me. I hated my teacher Miss Elsworth who had talked me into such a thing. Saying *Don't be silly Ingrid you know you can do it. It will be a challenge because you're a shy girl but how good you'll feel afterward. How proud. And your family, and your friends. Proud of you. Winning this year's poetry prize unprecedented in my memory that a sophomore should win. Of course you can't decline! Don't be silly you can practice beforehand. I can coach you. Aren't you proud? Why aren't you proud? I'm proud for you! You were my nominee. Don't let me down. And it's $50. Congratulations!*

Mother regarded me with worried eyes, she'd heard me up during the night using the toilet, my guts turned to liquid fire. I was obsessed the kids at the assembly would ridicule me, didn't I hear muffled laughter in the cafeteria, at my locker *Doll, Doll-girl, Hey Doll-girl: do me?* And the poetry I wrote was shit, and I knew it. Even the twelve-line poem that had won the poetry "competition." I should have screamed at Miss Elsworth to leave me alone for God's sake, I wasn't worthy of any prize didn't she know the fuck who I *was!*

I was ashamed that poems of mine had been printed in the school paper exposing INGRID BOONE to public wonderment and derision. In fact I was very excited, delirious. My life would be changed. All my teachers and Mr. Cantry the principal would see my poems, and all the kids, my enemies and my friends, for I did have friends, I counted my friends on my fingers compulsively during classes, or annotated their names in my notebook, X'ing out names, adding names, marking ☠ when somebody betrayed me. Of course, nothing was changed. There were three short poems in the paper and there were misprints in all three, even in the title of one of the poems so I could not show it to Mother even out of spite. Then I changed my mind and showed her. I was feverish seeing INGRID BOONE in print and was not sure if any of this was *real*. Mother frowned and read the poems two or three times. "You tell too much, Ingrid," Mother said finally. "A thing like this should scare you more."

Later, Mother said, "Being singled out can be a curse."

Her pronouncements were often mysterious. And more with each passing year. Her eyes all pupil, like she could see in the dark.

That morning Mother wanted to make me up, eager to make me *gorgeous* for my performance she and Mr. Dilts were going to attend together. First time in two years Chloe Boone had set foot in Mt. Ephraim High School though some of my teachers and the guidance counselor and Mr. Cantry had sent notes asking to see her. It was Class Day, final day of classes for the school year. Graduation for seniors was the following week.

"No thanks, Mother," I said. Peering into the bathroom mirror picking at a swelling above my left eye, it throbbed and itched and seemed to have something in its center, an insect's stinger maybe—I was trying to remove it with a tweezers. This was a delicate operation and Mother standing so close made me nervous.

And she was looking at me that way she had blinking like she'd been hurt, her daughter she loved so calling her MOTHER and no longer MOMMA. But I would not weaken. Ever again. Pushing past her into my bedroom where I lit a cigarette, my hands shaking. "Mother, please don't *look* at me. I'm fine!"

Mother said, "Ingrid, you are not 'fine,' your face needs making up. Your complexion is sickly, what's that on your forehead?—*I* can fix it. C'mon!" Clapping her hands brisk as a Girl Scout which was one of the weird roles she'd play mornings when she wasn't hungover. Smiling like the world is this blessed place like the night before, or whenever, she hadn't been in one of her moods wondering what the point of everything is, why the human race didn't give up after so many millennia. *Millennia* was a word Mother had gotten from TV, like *ecology* and *saturated fats*.

I shrank from Mother's touch with an exaggerated wince. She was dressed for Flora Wells' in a beige wool suit with white piping she had sewed herself and she exuded a sweet talcumy scent. Her face looked pretty good for a woman of thirty-three which was such an old age I knew I would never live that long. I stooped to scratch a rash on the back of my knee and Mother scolded, "Ingrid, damn it *stop*. It's just nerves." Slapping at my hand the way you'd slap at a child not wanting to hurt but out of vexation, disgust. Anything *just nerves* merits a slap.

Mother had to leave for Flora Wells' around the time I would be leaving for school and that time was fast approaching—8:10 A.M. The awards ceremony was at 4:30 P.M. and I could not comprehend how I would endure the intervening hours. There was the possibility of getting drunk, or high, my friends could help me out but if that happened how would I perform in front of an audience of over five hundred people? Another possibility was that I would run away, or kill myself. But I had not worked out any details. There was an older man I knew, in his late twenties, a trucker whose route was through Mt. Ephraim four times a week and we'd gotten together a few times and last time he'd said *C'mon with me Ingrid,* teasing but more than just teasing, like he truly meant it, his marriage was finished so I was thinking I could call him, I had his number, I could meet him in Port Oriskany, I could take a bus out of Mt. Ephraim by 10 A.M. Leaving a message for Miss Elsworth *So sorry I let you down, I know you can never forgive me & would not expect it.*

Mother was pushing close, I saw her nostrils widening she hoped to smell if I'd been sweating, and hadn't washed my underarms. Also she'd snatched up my pack of Newports and bummed one without so much as a word of request, or thanks. Shrewdly saying, seeing my sullen face, "You don't want me to come to the thing this afternoon, is that it?"

My heart kicked. I turned away. I'd known Mother would say this, these very words. I knew she would make it seem, if *she* didn't want to come, it was me who didn't want her to. She'd be doing me a favor by not coming! The selfish bitch.

I thought about the trucker, how his hands felt on me. He was an adult man, he had children. He would take care of me.

I was smoking my cigarette and my hands were

steadier. Calmly I said, "Do what you like, Mother. It's what you've always done."

"What does that mean?"

"What I said."

"What the hell does it *mean?*"

"*You* do what *you* want to do, and call it by some other name."

"What other name? What are you saying?"

"Mother, just leave me alone. I'm nervous about this afternoon. I'm *going*."

Now she was MOTHER and no longer MOMMA except in secret times of weakness it was like she was another person. Older, and her power lessened. Staring at me with these hurt eyes like *I was the cruel one of us*. Like *I* was reaching into her chest and squeezing her heart. I said, turning away, "I'm *going*. Don't come if you don't want to."

But Mother caught me then. Just a gentle touch of my arm, the way a guy once touched me a long time ago and he'd become my first lover and I still loved him though I forgot his name in my dreams of him. Mother said, "O.K., sweetie, but first let me make you *gorgeous*. Want to bet I can't?"

What could I do, I gave in. The truth was, I wanted to be *gorgeous* too.

Stole two of Mother's painkiller pills, swallowed down with lukewarm Coke. Cut my morning's classes at school and went instead to the Mt. Ephraim Public Library a weatherworn stone building beside the firehouse, frantically I searched through volumes of poetry looking for a poem I could read in place of my own, a poem that might be mistaken for a poem of mine except it would be a real poem, a worthy poem, by a real poet. I did not think this constituted theft, nor even *plagiarism*—I knew what *plagiarism* was. I was not thinking of that, at all. But only of finding something worthy to read to an audience, not insulting an audience with a poem by INGRID BOONE. Not just students would be at the assembly but all the teachers, my tenth-grade teachers and teachers I would have in the future, and Mr. Cantry the principal, and parents, the parents of my classmates, and Mother and Mr. Dilts—I could not read my poem to them, the poem I'd won a prize for was the most pathetic shit. There were words like *sorrow* and *yarrow* in it that rhymed by accident, there were words *perish of being* that made no sense. The subject was a pilot, a man in a small plane flying so high above the earth at night he'd lost his way, he was out of radio contact and his instruments were spinning because of electricity in the clouds and his gas tank was almost empty, all this crap was invented, I didn't know anything about flying a plane really, and a real pilot, *if there was one in the audience*, would laugh at my ignorance and expose me. The fancy cloud words *cirrus*, *cumulus*, *stratus* I'd copied out of a dictionary. And there was a line *a moment in a strange world* I'd stolen from a poem by Robert Frost not in our textbook. It amazed me that Miss Elsworth hadn't recognized the line. Wasn't she as smart as I'd thought? Or had she recognized it, and making me read the poem at the assembly was my punishment? Yet I could not comprehend how the woman I knew could be so calculatingly cruel for hadn't Miss Elsworth praised my writing and given me A's for the past two years I'd

been her student? But it might have been that the
other teachers on the awards committee had talked
her into the deception, or just possibly they had plotted
behind her back and deceived her into agreeing to
award the poetry prize to me in order that, at the
assembly, at the very end of the school year, INGRID
BOONE would be exposed and humiliated. And Miss
Elsworth would be exposed and humiliated, too! So
there was no choice but for me to find an authentic
poem by an authentic poet and copy it into my notebook to read at the assembly but my nerves were tight-
strung and the painkillers and cola-caffeine were
making my heart beat weirdly skipping every third or
fourth beat then racing to catch up so I was having difficulty just holding books and leafing through their
pages without dropping them *Help me! help me God!*
in whom I did not believe searching for a poem of
approximately the right length as mine and a poem I
could comprehend whose words I would be capable
of reading without stammering. I was "made up" for
the assembly and I was wearing a navy-blue dotted-
swiss dress Momma, I mean Mother had sewed for me,
a good dress, and nice shoes, and I was sweating and
breathing hard so the librarian poked her head
around the stacks to see what the hell I was doing,
hyperventilating at the back of the reference section,
and she asked do you need any help miss and I said
No! No thanks! I'm O.K. and she looked at me like she
was wondering why wasn't I in school, she took note
of my pretty-pretty dress and black ballerina flats worn
with actual stockings so I didn't look like myself at all
but another girl and possibly even a good girl and a
good student so she said well if you need any help

please let me know, and went away. Through a tall narrow window the sky pulsed and glared like a heartbeat. Every time I looked at my watch a gap of time was missing. It required two hours of leafing through anthologies some of them so heavy, their pages yellowed and cracked, books that had not been checked out of the library nor perhaps even glanced into in thirty years. So I believed I would be safe choosing poems from them. In a fever copying a dozen poems by poets whose names were vaguely familiar yet whose poems were not in our school text *William Blake*, *Samuel Taylor Coleridge*, *Elizabeth Barrett Browning*, *Dante Gabriel Rossetti*, *Thomas Hardy*, *A. E. Housman* but I left off their names because I would not be acknowledging the other poet. And as I copied these poems into my notebook in my handwriting it seemed almost the poems *were* mine, my inventions! I reasoned that, if a line by Robert Frost was not known to my English teacher, a poem by these older, less-read poets would not be known at all.

During this time my bites, rashes, pimples flared up like patches of kerosene touched by a match. There were many more than eleven now, there must have been twenty, or thirty! My face Mother had carefully made up was stiff and poreless with creamy Revlon foundation and a thick dusting of perfumy powder I knew I must not touch. I limited myself to scratching only what was hidden. Inside my clothes, inside my panties. The bites on my thighs were terrible. And the burning pebble-hard bite or pimple on the underside of my breast. The backs of my knees where three-inch-long welts were raised matching the grooves of my raking nails, and it was tricky to scratch through the nylon stockings without causing a run and maybe I did cause a run, I couldn't see. *Don't! don't* I was thinking as tentatively I touched my face—it was burning. Very cautiously like a blind person I touched the string of pimples at my hairline just lightly drawing my nails back and forth over them. Oh God this made them itch all the more. Terrible, terrible itching! It was like a guy touching the tip of his cock against me just the tip of the little ridge of flesh between my legs so stiff and aching and his breath so hot and quickened and the moaning in his throat he didn't hear *Oh! Jesus* and I would bite my lip hard enough to draw blood not wanting to come, not wanting it to happen, not like that, so exposed. Because I screamed and cried so, I could not help myself, and that scared them even the older guys sometimes, it was ugly to them, and gross, I understood that other girls were not so wild and help- less and grabbing so and of course the good girls did not do such things at all, it was not required of them. So I should not have touched the pimples on my fore- head, that was an asshole thing to do. Momma, I mean Mother had rubbed them with alcohol to soothe the itching then she'd rubbed moisturizer over my entire face before applying the foundation and until I'd touched it my face had been O.K. like a clay mask but now it was alive and throbbing with itching. The bump above my eye I'd removed the insect stinger from had swollen to twice its original size, and how it itched! But I didn't dare touch it because that would only make the itching worse. And if I began to scratch it would bleed through the makeup. And if I disturbed the makeup all Momma's, I mean Mother's efforts would be in vain for though sullen and red-eyed I did look O.K., you might say *pretty-pretty*, yeah even *gorgeous*, I was fifteen and with lipstick, a light shading of rouge on my cheeks, certain tricks of Momma's I could be made to look pretty good if you didn't look too close. It you didn't know I was Ingrid Boone.

By the time I finished copying the poems in my notebook scrawled and drunken-looking and my handwriting almost illegible it was after noon, I'd missed all my morning classes. And it was June 11, the final day of classes. But I was feeling better now. Even as I knew something terrible would happen, I was making a terrible mistake, I was feeling better. This was a frequent phenomenon and would characterize my life for years. Through the library window there was the same sky opaque and glaring like metal but you could imagine the sun behind it. I smiled, I was happy, almost. I'd saved a third painkiller for just before the assembly. Hadn't been realizing how I was scratching my itchy spots up and down my body except for my face and throat, raking my nails luxuriously and at all these points there was a burning sensation that might have been pain if I'd been registering pain which I was not. *It will be a challenge because you're a shy girl. How proud. And your family, and your friends. And it's $50. Congratulations!*

Before the awards assembly everyone in the program had to gather backstage at 4:30 P.M. and by this time I'd taken the painkiller and drunk three cans of Coke so my stomach felt full though I hadn't eaten anything all day, and bloated. And I'd been running to the restroom and peeing, having to pull down my panty hose I wasn't used to, and the itching on my thighs and belly so terrible I scratched and dug at my skin not giving a damn how the bites were bleeding, they were inside my clothes, and hidden. I hadn't yet decided which poem to read, the poem would have the title "Lost" because that was the title of the prize-winning poem by INGRID BOONE listed in the awards program and I could not change that. During my afternoon classes I'd been distracted looking through the poems and now backstage even as the assembly was about to begin I was still looking, standing off to one side as Mr. Cantry gave directions and not even pretending to listen so they noticed me, and Miss Elsworth said something to me but I didn't hear. Strange to me to be *backstage* behind the heavy velvet curtains, and to hear the noisy audience filing in, I was in a daze open-eyed like somebody hypnotized by the roaring churning rapids above a falls carried unresisting to the falls, and over. My heart was beating erratically and I could not seem to catch my breath though the pills had made me sluggish, my legs heavy. I was gripping sheets of torn-out notebook paper trying to make my decision. After today I would go to live with the trucker in Port Oriskany, I needed only to remember his last name, his first name was Mike. A trickle of sweat ran down my side beneath my dress and something was tickling-itching on my forehead I brushed at with my nails. By this time the assembly had begun. To my horror Mr. Cantry had pushed through the curtains and the audience quieted and he began the program by leading them in the Pledge of Allegiance his voice booming like a voice in a movie and I saw that we who were backstage were not spared but had to place our right hands over our hearts chant-

ing the familiar words like robots. And then there
was a brisk musical interlude, a prizewinning student
trumpeter accompanied by a student pianist, both
graduating seniors. And then a woman's amplified
voice, one of the senior teachers, the first of the
awards *notable achievement in student government*.
And then applause. A few whistles. It was a lively
assembly, the last of the year, and some of the boys
would be raucous, some might even be drunk, beer
smuggled into their lockers, a few of the girls even,
Ingrid Boone might've been one of them, not trapped
like I was, dragged closer and closer to the edge. It
washed over me then with a sickening horror that
Momma, I mean Mother would be here, she and her
man friend Mr. Dilts who was another woman's husband "separated" like Momma was "separated," and
my classmates would see her, and him. And I wanted
them to know that Momma was my mother so much
younger and better-looking than their mothers but I
didn't want them to think that Mr. Dilts was my father,
the idea filled me with revulsion. I scratched at my
forehead, I brushed my hair out of my eyes. Dropped
some of my papers and stooped to retrieve them and
someone was whispering, "Ingrid?"—it was Miss Elsworth staring at me appalled and handing me a tissue
I stared dumbly at and did not take and so delicately,
biting her lip Miss Elsworth dabbed at my forehead
above my eye where I must have been scratching and
started the bump bleeding without knowing what I
did. The tissue was dotted with blood—Miss Elsworth
crumpled it quickly in her hand as if it were shameful,
she whispered it might be better if I didn't touch my
face. But I was distracted, on the other side of the

curtain there was a roar of applause, and amplified voices, the athletic awards, an outburst of laughter, and more applause and whistles. The popular senior guys were out there receiving trophies, scholarship certificates. The president of the Mt. Ephraim Chamber of Commerce was giving a speech punctuated by jokes, laughter and applause. People backstage were pushing out through the curtains, others were returning flush-faced and grinning. In desperation I'd chosen a poem titled "Grief" whose author I did not know, one of the most obscure of the poems I'd copied so seemingly one of the most poetic, my lips were moving as I read through it without comprehension like a brain-damaged person. Miss Elsworth pushed out through the curtains to begin the literary announcements and her voice was reproduced backstage amplified, remote and scarcely recognizable. I thought *If Momma is not here, I will never love her again and I will never be hurt by her again.* My heart was pounding so hard I had difficulty hearing the first name announced which was that of a boy, a senior boy who'd been awarded the prize for fiction, and there was welcoming applause, and the boy's voice unexpectedly confident, even droll, as he read from his winning story, and at the conclusion there was laughter, and more applause. And then I heard Miss Elsworth call my own name—INGRID BOONE. The singular ugliness of that name had never struck me before. My legs had turned to lead, I could not move until someone nudged me, *Ingrid?—this way* it was kindly Mr. Cantry himself guiding me as I blundered into the heavy curtains, groped my way out onto the stage unprepared for the narrowness of the stage in front of the curtains and the brightness of the lights and the nearness of the audience—the first several rows so close, the faces of individuals vividly clear, their eyes and expectant expressions, so near! There had been a scattering of handclaps as my name was pronounced and I stared out seeing so many eyes on me, I had imagined this moment for weeks, had endured it how many sleepless hours yet I had always imagined the audience a vague blur like flooding water, a terrible presence yet without specific identity. But here were faces, here were faces of boys and girls I knew, boys and girls who knew me, I stood paralyzed as Miss Elsworth spoke of the annual poetry prize and the local poet who had endowed it and another time I heard my strange jarring name INGRID BOONE and felt very tired walking to the podium and unprepared for Miss Elsworth's smile and brisk handshake for when had I shaken hands with any adult before, or with anyone at all?—and she thrust at me a large stiff certificate with a gilt seal and an envelope and in my confusion I dropped some of my papers and had to stoop to retrieve them my face pounding with blood. The audience by now was completely silent. I might have been alone in the auditorium. Miss Elsworth disappeared, and I stood on tiptoe at the podium staring at something I held in my hand, I smoothed the wrinkled sheet of paper uncertain whether this was in fact the poem I'd finally chosen. I had intended to weave into the poem some of my own lines from "Lost" so that Miss Elsworth and anyone else who knew that poem would believe this to be a revision but I hadn't had time, or I'd forgotten. I had intended to announce the title "Lost" but that too slipped from my mind. Like a diver plunging into unknown water I began to read, staring at the words quivering in front of me I'd never seen before and in some cases could not pronounce but had to repeat and even then it was not certain that I had pronounced them correctly, I brushed at my forehead, dug my nails pushing my damp hair out of my eyes, couldn't catch my breath reading in a rapid then halting dazed fumbling voice— " 'I tell you, hopeless grief is passionless; / That only men incredulous of despair, / Half-taught in anguish, through the midnight air / Beat upward to God's throne in loud access / Of shrieking and reproach. Full desertness, / In souls as countries, lieth silent-bare / Under the blanching, vertical eye-glare / Of the absolute heavens. Deep-hearted man, express / Grief for thy dead in silence like death— / Most like a monumental statue set / In everlasting watch and moveless woe / Till itself crumble to the dust beneath. / Touch it; the marble eyelids are not wet: / If it could weep, it could arise and go.' " As I read I felt a trickle of blood run down the side of my face, I swiped at it with my hand and smeared it on my cheek, wiped harder then tried to ignore it, wanting only to get through the poem, to get through. By the time I finished, the audience was even more silent. There were scattered coughs. I stared out terrified at the rows of faces not knowing how to be released from their eyes. At last someone began applauding, it was Miss Elsworth herself somehow beside me, and all the audience joined in, so it was over, blindly I turned and followed Miss Elsworth through the curtains and so backstage breathing so quick and shallow I began to faint, Miss Elsworth and another woman asked did I want to lie down somewhere and I shook my head no! no I was all right, winced when they touched me as if their fingers burnt. Mr. Cantry was headed for me angry-looking but Miss Elsworth turned me aside, shoved another tissue into my hand whispering I should wipe my face which was bleeding along one cheek without my knowing it, or I'd forgotten. Behind my back making a gesture so Mr. Cantry should leave me alone. I thought *She knows. Knows I stole that poem. They all know.* But it wasn't certain they knew—was it? Probably they hadn't even heard the poem, most of it, my voice so rushed and faltering. Miss Elsworth was telling me not to be upset, I had done well. The other woman teacher, and others backstage, were telling me I had done well, and congratulating me. Miss Elsworth added maybe I should go to a rest room and wash my face?—would I like her to accompany me? I held the tissue to my forehead for the blood to soak in, it was shameful strangers should see my glistening blood, I didn't seem to hear Miss Elsworth or if I heard her her voice came from a distance and did not seem real. My head was heavy on my shoulders like a weight, my legs were numb and it was as if my feet were mired in mud. I thought I would go somewhere and lie down, a dark corner of the backstage maybe. There were piles of what looked like canvas. At the same time I knew this was wrong, like a dream when you are in a public place needing to pee. Mr. Cantry and the others were talking about me. Had I taken some *medication*, was that the problem. Part of the problem. Again Miss Elsworth seemed to be shielding me from Mr. Cantry, and from the others who were staring. We were moving toward the door and I handed the certificate and the envelope to her, I knew the envelope contained a check for $50 and Miss Elsworth said surprised, "What's this? It's yours, Ingrid," and I meant to say *I don't deserve it* but instead I said, "I don't want it," and Miss Elsworth protested, "It's yours, Ingrid," and I said, "No, I don't want it," and Miss Elsworth pushed at my hand like she was ashamed for me, "It's yours, it's made out in your name." There was a reception following the assembly where we were supposed to go, there would be a photographer from the local newspaper but I would not be there. And I would learn afterward that Mother had in fact been in the auditorium at the very rear but that she and Mr. Dilts had slipped away immediately after my appearance, that spectacle of Chloe Boone's daughter on a lighted stage before five hundred people with blood running down the side of her face *How could you Ingrid how could you God damn your soul to hell!* Mother and Mr. Dilts would not be at the reception of course. Would not meet the other parents, and my teachers, of course. I would not see Mother for a day and a half. Miss Elsworth was suggesting again that I wash my face, and maybe I should go home instead of to the reception. She would make my excuses for me. I whispered, "I'm so ashamed, Miss Elsworth, I'm sorry," but she was already backing away and hadn't heard me. I lifted my eyes to her face for the first time that day steeling myself for what I'd see, in the woman's eyes how she pitied me and how, if pity is strong enough, you won't be blamed.

A Woman
is Born to
Bleed

Laughed at me the way I was dancing, throwing my body to the beat. Slick with sweat and my long hair slapping. Like an eel being boiled one of the guys said. Maybe they weren't laughing at me, maybe it was just general laughing. These were hilarious times. These were happy times. They're vanished now, just litter and ripped-out wiring in houses marked NO TRES-PASSING THIS PROPERTY CONDEMNED but they were alive then, we all were.

I was high on two tabs of LSD, smashed so I didn't know my name. When I felt for my face, it was just nothing—smooth as a plate, and a sucking hole where the mouth had been. There were lights, lightbulbs turned to actual flames making the air quaver. The faces of my friends turned liquid like fluorescent rot running down their bones. I didn't judge! I saw it was the natural law of the universe. My own bones, my long slender forearm-bones, showed glimmering through my flesh like an x ray. My soul was the size of a pea rattling inside my hollow head. *Better bring her down,* somebody said. *She's gonna burst a blood vessel.* Another guy said, *Who the fuck is she?—who brought her here? She's just a kid.* Somebody called

somebody else *asshole*, *fuckhead*. There was a sound
of breaking glass like you'd imagine a xylophone.
Voices screaming but mine wasn't one of them. Where
my tank top was off my shoulder showing one of my
breasts, my skin oily like you'd imagine an actual eel,
somebody took hold and the fingers sunk in, right into
the flesh like it was putty. I laughed and pulled away
and what's he left with but the shoulder bone?—
laughed and laughed.

Later, it might've been another time, they sat me on
the knee, then it was the hard shinbone, of this guy Jax
who was Opal's boyfriend. *Giddyup! giddyup horsey!*
Jax was laughing. He was a shaved-head boy, with the
most beautiful eyes, and a mustache. His face shiny
like it'd been scrubbed and his big strong fingers had
bleached-looking nails, big blunt square-cut clean
nails like you never see on a man. Worked at Yewville
General and smuggled out pills and syringes in his
pockets. Baggy khakis. Wrapped in used Kleenex is the
trick Jax said, if anybody stops you they'd be disgusted
to examine a snot-dried Kleenex, right? Some of it he
sold but most he gave away to his friends, there was
such a strong love of friends for friends, these were
the people you'd die for. Opal laughed and squealed
making a face, she was fastidious about certain things
said aloud, given voice to, crude vulgar things, it was
O.K. to perform certain actions but not to speak of
them. Like going to the toilet, and she'd had an abor-
tion (I knew of this but Opal wasn't the one to tell me,
she'd have been furious to know people spoke of her
behind her back) but you'd never guess from how she
talked. Jax was a big boy, younger than Opal with
upper arms big as another man's thighs. And that

sand-colored mustache he was always chewing, like it helped him to think. I wanted him to like me, though. All of them, Opal's friends. There was Opal's ex-husband, too, people were scared of, not to his face exactly but he'd been eight months at Red Bank, a drug deal gone sour so he had certain grudges to repay. Somehow, that was understood and accepted. Jax was my special friend I'd thought, the way he smiled calling me *sweetheart*. And Opal would laugh and kiss me like I was some discovery of her own. *Isn't she! She is!*

Opal liked to kiss me in the beginning, the way Momma did years ago. Now she was Mother, not Momma. We fought all the time.

Begging Jax to let me go, it hurt me between the legs, my tender parts between my legs, I was wearing white shorts, and thin panties underneath. It'd been a hot summer day but now cold in the night and my legs pimpled with goose bumps and insect bites and scabs and bruises but nobody could see, it was too dark. I was sort of in love with Jax and this was my punishment maybe. *Giddyup baby!* Jax was saying. And everybody laughing, the look on my face maybe—I'd be trying to smile, trying not to show hurt, or that I was scared, sometimes that's funny in others' eyes. And Jax so big, my hands hidden inside his gripped tight so you could see just my wrists and no hands at all. I begged him let me go but it was loud in the room, in all the rooms they were partying, a speaker blaring rock music so loud you couldn't hear except for the heavy downbeat, the pulse, vibrations in everybody's bones like an earthquake. Tried to slide off Jax's shinbone and he'd grab me and position me pumping his crossed leg like a seesaw. Sometimes when you let them do what they want to do and don't try to stop them the evil energy runs through them like an electric shock. And it's over. The shine on Jax's face like something hot inside his skin pushing out. And his eyes. *Giddyup horsey! Baby-horsey!* Pumping his leg faster and faster and finally I started to cry and Opal came over and grabbed Jax's bald head in both her hands laughing telling him to stop.

I wanted them to like me, so badly. And this was one of my secrets from Mother who didn't have a clue what I was doing, all that summer staying with a cousin in Yewville, working at a fruit stand on the Sha-heen Road.

Selling fruit, pint baskets, quart baskets, bushel baskets. Tomatoes, pears, peaches, apples, cantaloupes, the smell of the cantaloupes so strong, the rear of the stand where the overripe melons were tossed, buzzing yellow jackets, flies, the smell of the rotting fruit, so the smell of cantaloupe would sicken me, and make me angry God knows why, all my life. Try to eat it, are you kidding?—right now, remembering, I'm nauseated.

Jax let go, and forgot me, in one minute they can forget you so you know no harm's meant. It was hard for me to walk without doubling over. Like my insides were hurt. But I'd be smiling, I had this smile people said was so sweet, Opal touched my face sometimes staring at me like you'd stare into a mirror. I was crazy for Opal and later on, hearing what happened to her, I just wouldn't think of it at all, I had the power to make my mind go blank, that's always in your power. That night is confused in my memory like so many. I didn't

have sex with anybody, any of the guys, I went away
crying, the pain scary like I'd been pounded there,
between my legs I wasn't even sure what it was called
except *vagina*, wasn't sure what that meant exactly,
was it the whole thing, *reproductive organ* the biology
textbook called it, or just the outside of it, there was
uterus too, *womb*, the woman Mother worked for,
owned a fancy women's clothing store in Mt. Ephraim,
Flora Wells—she had *uterine cancer*, an operation
and some treatments but in a few years she'd be dead.
I went into the bathroom trying to pee and there was a
numbness like needles, and burning. And next day
when I woke up wrapped in a blanket on the front
porch, it was an upstairs porch overlooking the
cracked sidewalk, already it was afternoon of whatever
day and I'd missed hours of work and had a hard time
getting to my feet my head was so heavy, my eyes out
of focus like trying to see under water. When I went to
the toilet this time the pain was like fire, and a knot
deep in my belly, and I saw it, the blood, in the toilet
bowl, and freaked calling Opal's name, just freaked
seeing the swirls of blood in the water, thin and
curling, streaks of red like long thin worms swimming
languidly and Opal came in and grabbed me to quiet
me, calling me *baby*, *sweetheart*, saying I was just
having my period, that's all. I was trembling, couldn't
seem to stop, and my teeth chattering, I told Opal it
was my first time, it hadn't ever happened to me
before, I was talking fast and nervous and Opal asked
if I was serious, this was my first?—looking at me like I
had to be lying. Standing there half naked my legs
bruised and scabby and my knees bent, like my body
was made of something brittle like ice that would

shatter if I moved the wrong way, and Opal asked hadn't my mother prepared me, and I lied and said no, and Opal said she had some Tampax she'd give me, and one of Jax's codeine tablets would take care of the cramps. Saying getting your period is no big deal, it's great news usually you're not pregnant. Saying *It's just a fact of life, baby, like any other. A woman is born to bleed.*

Too Young

I was in love with a guy about fifteen years older than me, my first time living with a man on my own. Downtown Port Oriskany in this hotel for transients we'd rent a room by the week because we didn't know our plans exactly. How things would work out, certain connections of his pending, from practically one hour to the next sometimes it can change, your entire life. I'd left a note for my mother *Don't bother to look for me. Good-bye.* This guy I was crazy for, and his ex-wife was a problem. She was a junkie, she wasn't in control. And turning up a few miles away from us, where we thought we'd shook her. My boyfriend was scared of her saying she's the kind of maniac to get hold of a gun and blow you away and then herself and she'd die happy. A smile on her face. Once she'd almost killed their little boy ten months old at the time banging his head against a tub, he'd had to take the child to Syracuse emergency and *he* almost got arrested, child battering, there's a state law you get reported if injuries look suspicious.

I asked, Then what happened?

He said, Nothing. I didn't get arrested. I made some explanations and it was O.K.

I said, I mean what happened to your son?

He said, shrugging, looking at me the way he'd do when I was getting on his nerves, Timmy's O.K. He's with her mother now. Up in St. Lawrence.

I said, Was he badly hurt? When you took him to the hospital, I mean.

Why I'd keep pushing like this, I don't know.

He said, You don't want a kid of your own, I sure hope. Is that what all this weird shit is getting at?

This scared me. I backed off from him right away.

No, I said. I'm too young to have a baby.

Yeah, he said, eyeing me. But, you know, you're not.

Man Crazy

Fell in love with the look of a man in a Navy seaman's jacket. A face I didn't know, just the rough edge of it, as he was turning, and dark stiff longish hair like something trailing in water. That was a summer night in a tavern on the Cassadaga River, one of those misty nights smelling of rain that are always the same night, and everything to come. You know you're happy, your heart's gonna burst. Another time there was a guy crossing a street in Port Oriskany near the university, and I was in a car with somebody and it was a light rain too, a steamy hazy rain and the guy was running, his legs muscular and bare in shorts, and a T-shirt glaring white in the traffic lights. Dark skinned, and I'd never been with a dark-skinned man, they were maybe scared of me, so blond and so hungry. *Get away from me, girl. You too young* one of them said to me once, laughing and backing off like seeing something in my face I never knew was there.

Later, I would be Dog-girl. But the look of Dog-girl was in my face already, some guys could see it.

Also in Port Oriskany this time I'm thinking of, it was so sweet. It was my first time that sweet. Always I'd known what you were supposed to feel, a guy high and deep inside, and slow going, and easy, so you wouldn't ever guess you could be lonely again, ever in your life. Just remembering such a time, I mean.

There was a man in the Empire Hotel bar where I'd come sometimes. A pink neon sign COCKTAILS COCKTAILS COCKTAILS winking on and off in the front window. And back behind the bar if there was a certain bartender there, an older guy I got along with real well, there'd be a German shepherd dog stretched out sleeping, his head on his paws, he'd remind me of Happy, this dog that belonged to my daddy a long time ago. So there was this man, and he's with a woman. And she's wearing a yellow-check jacket and a black skirt and open-backed high heels, glamorous like a woman in an old TV movie, he's wearing a white shirt, the sleeves rolled up to his elbows, a loosened necktie like he's warm from drinking, and his sport coat folded on the bar stool next to him. And he's nodding, like he's impatient, or he's heard it before, listening or maybe not listening to the woman's voice, he's staring over her shoulder and his drink in his hand, a mixed drink, and I'm like a dancer moving slow and each instant calculated as I bring myself into the man's line of vision and, Jesus! my breath is knocked out of me, this guy is so good-looking—the set of his eyes, the heavy eyebrows, the mouth that's fleshy but hard-looking—his hair that's a little too long, curling up by his collar, and in wetted tendrils across the top of his head where it's going thin—his jaw that's dark, he hasn't shaved for a day or two. I see him, he's thirty-five maybe, and he's seeing me now. And the look of him pierces me like a knife blade, O Jesus I feel faint, scared as hell and beginning to tremble and my mouth so dry I can't swallow.

And if I wait in the lobby of the seedy Empire Hotel this man will come out in a few minutes. I'll count my pulse beat, waiting. He'll be alone, he's left the woman waiting at the bar, he's on his way to the men's room he's told her, or maybe to make a telephone call. And he'll see me, and he'll be smiling. And his eyes dark. And he'll come over to where I'm standing, and he'll tell me his room number if he's staying in the hotel. He'll give me his business card, if he has a business card. *Maybe we can get together for a drink later tonight?* he'll say. And I'm looking him in the face, looking up at him because he's taller, I'm not afraid to look at him direct, my eyes are bright with staring so hard it's that intense. And I'm trembling, my fingertips like ice. Always it's that intense, and always for the first time ever in your life, you'd swear. *Yes* I'll tell him. *Maybe. I'd like that.*

I don't play games, I never did. Crazy for men they say it's really your own daddy you seek. I hope this is so, maybe someday I'll find him.

The Cock
of Satan

Tell me of your life you said.

Mostly, it wasn't mine.

That first time I saw Enoch Skaggs, and he saw me. Cutting his motorcycle in the street, so there was this silence. Waves of silence washing in. Removing his reflector sunglasses to stare at me. Like he knew me already, had identified me. The way a man can make his claim. If he has the power, and Enoch Skaggs had the power. I saw him, I stood there in the street my bones melting, whatever my life was up until that moment melting, gone.

Like a razor's swipe so fast you're bleeding before you even know you've been cut.

He summoned me, and I went to him. *My name is Enoch Skaggs, you may have heard of me.* In his biker's leather, his wild dark hair, tattoos on his muscled arms. His eyes the clearest blue of any eyes I had ever seen. Blue of the empty sky you can fall and fall into forever. Blue reflected in the ice-locked river glittering like mica so sharp it hurts your skin. The first time Enoch Skaggs made love to me he warned he was icy-cold, beware all who touch one who is icy-cold without caution for they will be burnt. The cock of Satan is icy-cold and it was out of that cock that Enoch Skaggs was sired.

Lost Kittens

Slow and cruising the highway north of Chautauqua Falls in Enoch Skaggs' van when I was eighteen years old and living in different places with different people, taking money where I could, working part-time in the county clerk's office and it wasn't *my life* but just *a life* that seemed to be happening, like weather. Enoch Skaggs at the wheel of the bullet-colored van, in his dark glasses even at twilight, sharp-eyed, watchful, a hunter seeking his prey. And Flatfoot beside him, Gem and Zed and me in the rear, Ingrid's their girl tonight, I'm being initiated. Cruising the highway past the Chautauqua County Farm Service Bureau, across the river and past the railroad crossing at the hill, the granaries looking like cardboard cutouts at this time of evening, the neon-lit Days Inn, Cinema X, prefab buildings FOR SALE, the Falls Shopping Center where Enoch Skaggs turns in, now looping through the parking lot slow and watchful at five miles an hour. *Who am I, am I Ingrid?*—sitting tense and erect in my skeleton staring at halos around my friends' heads, blue flames licking at Enoch Skaggs' hair, the air is charged as air before an electric storm and the sky is shifting every moment, every second ceaseless as the

river. Serpents and dragons in those clouds. Sometimes the teasing lineaments of Satan's very face.

People cause their own sorrow my daddy once said.

Why then feel guilty, why feel responsible?—you
aren't even Ingrid Boone anymore, you're *Dog-girl*.
Enoch Skaggs has promised that as long as I do his
bidding, as long as I'm his sweet baby girl I'm under
his protection, I won't be hurt. Keeps me supplied
with the drugs I need. Like other girls, women of his
who belong to Satan's Children, wearing their gold-
stud insignia, their X tattoos. But none of these others
are here tonight in Enoch Skaggs' van with the
window at the rear painted over in black, *Dog-girl is
the chosen one.*

Out of the tape deck, heavy metal is blaring. That
rock music you don't need to listen to, to hear.
POUNDING POUNDING POUNDING in your bones.

Driving at five miles an hour along the diminished
rows of cars. The Falls Shopping Center is mostly
closed at this time of evening but there's this solitary
girl about fifteen years old walking quick and unsee-
ing, head lowered smoking a cigarette in short puffs
like she's pissed about something, halfway across the
parking lot her girlfriends are talking to some young
guys and she's going home and they don't seem to
notice, or don't give a damn. "There she is," Enoch
Skaggs says quietly. "Go into action, Dog-girl."

Dog-girl's just teasing, Enoch Skaggs is so wild for
me. Doesn't want his friends to guess.

So I climb down out of the van. The pavement is
hard, grease-stained, I'm wondering is this a dream,
where are my shoes?—I'm barefoot, stepping on broken

glass. My eyes are burning like I've been staring into the sun. Or haven't slept in a long long time.

The van moves off. I'm smiling at the girl, I walk up to her like we're friends, we're sisters. I have this new confidence now, like fiery mercury injected in all my veins. I have the idea that my eyes might be phosphorescent. I don't want to scare this girl so I keep my smile in control. I can't reveal the happiness in my heart. "Hi!" I say to the girl, and she cuts her eyes at me like she's wondering should she know me, she says uncertainly, "Hi," I see she's a sweet-looking girl not pretty but with a clear soft skin, pear-sized breasts in a snug little T-shirt, denim cutoffs, brown hair tied back in a ponytail. "Kind of hot tonight, isn't it," I'm so friendly she's got no choice but to smile at me, the van is circling at a distance, a weekday night at the shopping center and there's the unlit area behind JCPenney where trucks make their deliveries and pickups and it's out of the range of vision of the girl's friends who aren't watching her who've forgotten her in any case, so I'm pointing in that direction, "Know what?—I found some lost kittens over there!—I don't know what to do," my hands are trembling if you looked closely, my eyes have that speedy glow, the girl is staring at me smiling like she doesn't understand so I'm thinking maybe I'm not speaking loud enough? or speaking too fast? or is it a dream, I'm not speaking at all but only thinking, "Do you love kittens?—I *love* kittens! I'm worried they'll starve to death all alone over there, the mother cat was killed by a car." Blinking tears out of my eyes it's so real to me, it's like Enoch Skaggs is whispering in my ear the right words, *all you need is the right words and you got her.* "Oh

God! Kittens? Where are they?" the girl says, her eyes
wide, so I show her, walking together like old friends,
like sisters about the same height, she's a little heavier
than I am, my legs and arms thin and hers smooth,
sleek with soft down on her arms, hurrying toward the
rear of JCPenney and in the corner of my eye there's
the bullet-colored van turning, circling back. The van's
name is *Thunderhead* but that name is nowhere
visible. I tell the girl how I happened to hear mewing
and went over there and discovered the kittens, saw
just two of them at first, tiny tiger kittens, with white
markings, so tiny you could hold them both in the
palm of your hand, then I saw a third kitten, and a
fourth, all of them mewing, so hungry and lost, and I
ask the girl what's her name and she says, "Gayellen
Cruse," and I'm laughing, " 'Gayellen Cruse'—no kidding! I had a best friend once, Gail Ellen," and she
asks, "What's your name?" and we're passing a single
light on a tall post making a hissing sound like something is broken in the bulb and leaking out, moths and
gnats circling the light beating against it, and I'm
smiling because I'm walking on glass in my bare feet
and by Enoch Skaggs' directive *There is no pain to be
felt* telling the girl, "I'm new here, my family just
moved here, I'll be a senior at the high school next
month and I don't know anybody," and the girl says,
"No kidding!—I'll be a junior," and we're almost
around the corner in the shadowy place and the van is
idling not far away, you wouldn't notice it unless you
were looking for it, but the girl isn't looking for it, the
two of us peering at the ground calling "Kitty! Kitty-
kitty-kitty!" It's a matter of seconds now. The girl
won't have time to scream but if she does the guys will

have dragged her into the rear of the van and somebody's hand hard over her mouth and Enoch Skaggs
turning and exiting the parking lot at a steady speed,
it's like it has happened already, the clock has run
ahead. *No pain to be felt. No pain.* The air is soft and
thick in mild rippling waves, the sky has gone darker,
back of JCPenney it's almost night. Why isn't the girl
suspicious, why does she trust me? Suddenly I'm
pissed at her, dumb bitch you deserve what's coming.
She's even tossed away her cigarettes so intent on
finding the lost kittens, "Kitty-kitty-kitty?" I'm close
behind her, my mouth is going and my eyes burning
in their sockets and I hear the van approaching behind
us and my hand leaps out, my fist punches her soft
shoulder, in this low furious voice I'm saying, "You,
get out of here! Run like hell!" and the girl turns her
face to me, her face of absolute astonishment like the
inside of a mollusc whose shell has been prized off,
I'm smiling grinning so the men in the van can't guess
what I'm saying, "I'm not your friend, I'm an emissary
of Satan! Get out of here, run like hell! Go on!" my
voice lifting to almost a scream, and in that instant the
girl sees the van, she's wide-eyed as a terrified child
shaking her head *no no*, turns, begins to run, her
shoulder bag falls to the ground and she doesn't stop
to retrieve it, damn dumb bitch running for her life,
running clumsily, now calling for her friends, crying
out somebody's name. And the van has swerved
around, headed in the opposite direction, rushing
from the lot out to Route 11.

Stumbling barefoot along the highway. *Dog-girl* of
no more consequence than *dog shit*. They'd left me,

Enoch Skaggs and the others and the soles of my feet
were bleeding now, could feel the pain such pain I
was grateful for knowing I deserved it. I wasn't crying
but dry-eyed. Traffic rushed by throwing up grit and
stink in my face, I breathed it in knowing it was what I
deserved. Or if I was crying it was more like coughing,
a fit of laughing that turns to choking on your own
phlegm you have to lean over, spasms ripping through
you till finally you manage to spit it out, a slick greeny
clot like something alive. The warm buzz of happiness
in all my veins was faded like neon tubing when the
light's switched off, I had a sweating headache and my
bowels ached, my shit hardened to concrete. You're a
druggie somebody warned me your shit will harden to
concrete. But it was just something that happened,
like weather.

A few cars, pickups slowed, men yelled out to ask if
I needed help if I wanted a ride, a station wagon with
a woman and kids but I waved them away. *No! leave
me alone!* and they did and I'd gone how many miles
on Route 11 not even knowing which direction,
should have been headed back into town but instead
was headed north where there was nothing but
country for a long distance, steep hills, the foothills of
the mountains, now the sun was entirely gone and the
sky layered in dense boiling clouds and the booming
voice at the underside of the earth the voice out of the
whirlwind you can't hear except at such times a voice
of such rage like rolling thunder and I felt the first hot
hissing raindrops, I saw with derision the wan figure,
tattered pale-blond hair falling between her shoulder
blades halfway down her back, her downlooking face,
dark shirt and bleached cutoffs and the thin legs, bare

feet no longer flinching with pain but numbed to it, on the edges of dissolution, extinction. *Tell me where I can come to get you Ingrid, oh please don't hang up* but he'd taken the receiver from me, my fingers unresisting.

Finally the van pulled up beside me and Zed reached out grabbed my hair, dragged me into the back of the van cursing me and Enoch Skaggs gunned the motor and the tires squealed, threw up gravel. Zed, Gem, Flatfoot beat me with their fists yelling *Cunt! Stupid cunt! What the fuck did you tell her!* and I tried to say I hadn't told her anything, she just got scared and started to run and it wasn't my fault but they didn't believe me or if they believed me it didn't make any difference they were cursing me, shaking my head gripping my hair in their fists like they wanted to tear it out, blood in a warm trickle from my nose and my mouth and that pissed them all the more beating me till Enoch Skaggs driving the van yelled for them to stop, called them fuckheads ordering them to stop, to leave Dog-girl for him. And they did.

Satan's
Children

There are epochs when God departs the world of mankind, and in His departure Satan reigns. This is destiny and no one is to blame for living in such epochs.

Sometimes the summons from Enoch Skaggs came so strong, I heard his voice when I was miles from him. *Dog-girl! Dog-girl, come.* The morning of the sacrifice of the guy called Gem was such a morning.

An empty bleached-blue sky falling upward forever, just to cast your eyes upward was to see how far away God was. How He had ceased to hear.

I heard Enoch's voice and thought *I'm so afraid.*

I heard Enoch's voice and thought *He will take my fear and annihilate it. He will deliver me to be born again in his sight.*

So I did not go to my job in the county clerk's office where I was "Ingrid Boone" and where they liked me or believed they did. Instead I went on foot to this guy I knew to ask him please drive me to the house on Dundee Road.

How did we speak of it. We would speak of it as just *the house* or maybe the women would call it *the family house, the family place.* But never to outsiders.

Artie, fattish sunburned face and squinched up

eyes, in his late twenties and already going bald, stared at me like I was involving him in some crime. And Artie liked it or thought he might like it. A long time ago he'd been a big deal at the high school playing football, now he lived with his parents and worked gas pumps and he knew rumors of Satan's Children, knew they were bikers just possibly dealing in drugs, living out on the Dundee Road. So there was glamour to it. And Artie knew the name Skaggs because he'd known a cousin of Enoch's from Marsena, a man my father used to know. So staring at me he said he couldn't get away till noon and could I wait that long or was I going to get somebody else to drive me?

So badly he wanted to be the one. Thinking maybe Enoch Skaggs would summon *him.*

I was shivering in the warm sun. Hugging myself, my skinny rib cage, breasts, the summons from Enoch Skaggs was vibrating in me so hard. Like after sex when you're knocked out. Can't remember anything that has happened any more than a baby could. Artie came close to me breathing in that short quick way of a guy fucking you in his head while he's keeping it all level, practical minded. "Hey Ingrid? C'n you wait till noon?"

This was at the Sunoco station on Route 11. Just outside town. An old beat-up kitchen chair by the cigarette machine in the owner's office where I sat waiting till Artie could get free. A calendar sun bleached on the wall from some other year, a woman in a bikini winking at me like we were sisters. I thought *It never makes any difference what year it is. Every year is the same year.* Shut my eyes to get to that state where I

wasn't there and I wasn't anywhere except preparing
to come to Enoch Skaggs who had summoned me. In
that way of his like the river you see moving slow in
the sun in broad sweeping waves you wouldn't guess
are so powerful and so dangerous if you waded into
the water, laughing like a child if you waded into it
and lost your footing and fell where it was over your
head. *Dog-girl. Dog-girl. Dog-girl.* He'd sent me away
and it was his right to summon me back.

In the county clerk's office I was "Ingrid Boone" an
assistant file clerk and I was in disguise. But in the Sunoco station, word got out I was waiting in the office, the
owner wasn't there just the mechanics and guys hanging out and Artie who'd told them about me—they
knew who I was. So they'd come to stare at me through
the dirty window separating the office from the interior
of the garage. They'd mouth certain words to me, grin
and make gestures and I turned away half shutting my
eyes, ignoring them for I was Enoch Skaggs' girl, no
one other than Enoch Skaggs could touch me. One of
them rapping on the window and I wouldn't look and
he opened his pants and jacked off in my face except
the glass was between us and I never looked nor gave
any sign of acknowledgment for I was *Dog-girl! Dog-
girl!* under Enoch Skaggs' protection.

Opening my eyes at last and there was nobody there,
they'd given up on me. The glass was smeared and snot
clotted, glistening with his cum I refused to see.

Refused to give any of you observing me the
satisfaction.

This old farmhouse Enoch Skaggs brought the
family to live in, on the Dundee Road—the previous

owners had been an elderly couple and when the wife died in her sleep the husband left the body where it was in the bed and slept in the kitchen for two or three years before he died, too, and neighbors eventually found him. So there was the one corpse, the man, frozen upright beside the wood-burning stove where the fire had gone out in sub-zero cold; and the other corpse, the woman, at the back of the house decomposed in patches like soft leather sticking to bone and part melted into the filthy bedclothes, no eyes, nose, or ears remaining but everybody spoke of her fine long hair, yellow-white hair long as a girl's hair they said that looked as if it'd just been combed. Nobody could be located to buy such a place, or rent it, so the land was sold at auction by the county and there came Enoch Skaggs to make a bid. Enoch Skaggs had a scorn of such superstition of course! *Death is always with us, Death is our ally.*

It was told in the family of how Enoch had handed over fifty-three hundred dollars in cash for the property. And nobody dared to ask him any questions.

As he'd paid, too, for *Thunderhead* and a new license plate—twelve hundred dollars in cash. And no questions asked.

Now the house and barns (except for the charred silo) are all burnt rubble and weeds and signs warning NO TRESPASSING ORDER OF CHAUTAUQUA CO. SHERIFF. But that is not what I see. So real in my head as if I'm there now, it's right in front of me! Back a lane about a quarter-mile and hardly more than a motorcycle trail through the weeds so Artie's pickup bounced and scraped and Artie was cursing to himself, sweat popping out in shiny beads on his face like he was more frightened than he knew. I sat with my fists on my bare knees and my insides tight as coiled snakes. Staring straight ahead and not knowing *Is Enoch Skaggs summoning me to love or to a test? To put my love to a test. To see is Dog-girl strong enough, worthy enough.*

And seeing the house again, that I'd been expelled from in such scorn, I was ashamed, my eyes ached with the sight.

That house. Where eleven of them would die. And Enoch Skaggs would die defending his honor.

Nobody had pictures of the house before the raid and the fire, the newspaper photos were all afterward. But I remember. It was like any other old farmhouse in the foothills above Chautauqua Falls, built how many decades ago before any of Satan's Children were born, and weatherworn and paintless like the barns and the tar-paper roof sagging, the brick chimney beginning to collapse upon itself. I can see the grain of the wood in sharp vertical lines like veins or nerves. I can see the windows so narrow, without shutters, mended in plastic strips, torn and flapping in the wind. That sad sound of thin plastic flapping, fluttering. All night you'd hear it, all day and all night in the wind. There were patches of moss bright as green neon growing out of the drainpipes. Inside, there were just five rooms counting the unfinished attic where you couldn't stand up straight even in the center. And the cellar had an earthen floor and a cistern but no furnace, the house was heated by two wood-burning stoves, there was a rusty hand pump at the kitchen sink, no indoor plumbing, the outhouse of unpainted rotted boards was at the top of a hill beyond the barnyard and down the length of that hill was marshy sewagey earth draining stinking shit and piss where in warm weather thousands of flies, some of them big as bumblebees, buzzed so crazed and loud it was like a thousand people murmuring excitedly together. Like the buzzing of lost souls one of the women said, maybe it was Dog-girl who said this. Or maybe Enoch Skaggs himself.

Waking hearing this buzzing MMMMZZZZMMMZZZZ inside my skull not knowing what it was, an acid trip or only just real life where I was living now, where I would call home.

The *place of bones* that was the family's secret of all secrets.

The burial ground unknown to any but the family, marked by rocks dragged from the fields in the formation of a big X—each side of the X measuring *three times seven feet* (which was Enoch Skaggs' decree)— this was on the far side of the barnyard from the outhouse, facing north in a stand of scrub beech where years ago there'd been a pasture. You could not see the *place of bones* from the driveway. Nor any of the rocks, some of them boulders weighing hundreds of pounds. For the X was to be seen and comprehended only from the air. A sign of Enoch Skaggs' *secret affiliation* as he called it. In the weeks and months to come there would be many photographs of the burial ground and TV footage, taken from helicopters, still the trees made it hard to see the actual shape of the X. And you could not really see it from the ground for the perspective was wrong. You would suppose those were just rocks scattered in a field gone to weeds, like any other field in this area.

Artie was driving his pickup slow, out of respect
and caution. Maybe he'd begun to wonder should he
be here at all. Should he have wanted to drive Ingrid
Boone out to see her friends. Seeing on the left as we
approached the house the guys' Harley-Davidsons and
cars and the bullet-colored, rust-splotched van *Thunderhead*, the rear window painted black. And piles of trash,
tires and auto scraps. And on the right an ancient apple
orchard—fantastic shapes of limbs twisted and bent and
broken from windstorms exposing the flesh of the inner
wood, that sad crippled look of fruit trees left to ruin.
In the winter a maze of twigs covered in snow like lace
and in summer thousands of bagworm-sacs in what
remained of the leaves and here and there wizened
apples offering themselves to be eaten.

Artie braked the pickup to a halt at the end of
the drive. He was breathing hard and quick as if he'd
been running. A scrawny black Labrador on a chain,
Enoch's dog Jackal, began to bark excitedly. Enoch
Skaggs himself stood on the sagging front porch of the
house watching us—just standing there. So you realized he'd been there all along watching as Artie drove
up. In his black satin vest with nothing beneath except
gold chains and his fiery tattoos and grizzly chest hair.
His low-slung jeans, kidskin boots, open-fingered
leather gloves and hair like an Indian's, dead black
straggling to his shoulders. Enoch Skaggs was a big
man, over six feet tall and weighing maybe two hundred twenty pounds with much weight in his torso so
he'd stand with legs apart, knees slightly bent like a
man bearing a precious burden. Even when he was
standing still looking calm and sleepy-eyed there was a

dangerous air to him like a snake prepared to strike, and you wouldn't know in which direction.

"Christ, is that him?"—Artie whispered.

It was not to me Artie spoke, nor even to himself. The words seemed taken from him, uttered in awe and in fear.

In that instant of Artie braking his pickup, and Enoch gazing at him with no more expression on his face than a rock would have, I saw a quick dream of Artie's, poor asshole Artie imagining he'd be buddies with Enoch Skaggs, driving a Harley-Davidson with the guys and sharing drugs and women, hooked up with big-time dealers out of Port Oriskany—I saw this, and almost could have laughed. And this before Flatfoot pushed open the screen door to join Enoch Skaggs, holding a rifle pointed at Artie in that easy cradling way the guys had, like a rifle or a shotgun was a baby to fit in the crook of your arm.

"Oh Jesus."

Artie whimpered like a kid. Thinking, yeah he'd made the worst mistake of his life driving out the Dundee Road.

A nod from Enoch Skaggs and I climbed down quick from Artie's pickup. Never even thanked Artie.

It was a sign of his *powers of mind* as he called them that Enoch Skaggs showed no surprise that I was there. He'd summoned me in his thoughts to return to the family and so it could be no surprise that I had returned. Nor that a stranger was the means of bringing me back.

"Dog-girl, get inside."

Enoch Skaggs scarcely looked at me. Yet I could see the pity in his face, and compassion.

My legs moved beneath me. In a blaze of light ascending the porch steps that were made of concrete blocks. Flatfoot was humming in that way of his stroking the long smooth barrel of the .22 like it was his cock, his left eyelid drooping where he'd been hit and the eyeball threaded with blood like a marble; gaze dropping to my feet and bare legs rising swiftly and his expression empty as Enoch Skaggs' so you would never know what he was thinking. I had to pass close between these men blinded and trembling as if passing close between two columns of upright flame the mere touch of which could destroy. Yet Enoch Skaggs did touch me—reached out, took my wrist and turned it just enough to hurt, to wake me if I needed waking and to propel me into the house. *You are mine, Dog-girl. And now put to the test.*

Went into the house, close to fainting my heart pumping so hard. I was home! Home. A strong familiar smell of burnt grease, rancid food and scorch from the kitchen and the earthy-mildewed stink of the old house, a smell of soiled bedclothes, blankets, towels. There was Jackal's anxious barking and there was the men's voices out front, the way guys go at one another, teasing, bantering, laughing, and always the threat beneath. Prepared myself for the *crack!* of the rifle for it was a sound I'd been hearing all my life. Enoch Skaggs was questioning Artie, and Flatfoot joined in, kidding around asking Artie who are you, fat boy? You a cop, fat boy? You Dog-girl's boyfriend, fat boy?—the name *Dog-girl* unexpected and sweet to my ears. And Artie tried to laugh to show he understood this was just joking, Flatfoot's rifle barrel trained on him was just a joke, these two bikers were possibly testing him, playing with him a little before releasing him. Artie was saying he wasn't no cop for sure, he worked at the Sunoco station in town, maybe they'd seen him, he'd pumped gas for them more than once, hey he'd just wanted to do the girl a favor driving her out. I was listening inside the door, my heart beating quick and hard *Don't shoot Artie, please! Artie is my friend* but then the voice turned mean *Kill him! He jerked off in my face.*

They kept poor asshole Artie in the driveway for ten minutes like that. In his pickup behind the wheel sweating in terror he's going to die. No way out, no way forward or back before Flatfoot could fire. Some other guys came to join them seeing what the yelling and laughing was, what Enoch and Flatfoot were up to, the asshole in the pickup was a ball they kicked between them. And Jackal barking, whimpering like if they'd only turn him loose, he'd tear out the asshole's throat. Poor Jackal they kept half starved.

Finally they said for Artie to get the fuck out, and don't look back, and I heard Artie turning the truck around in the driveway, the gears grinding. And I heard the truck being driven away. And still I was waiting for the *crack!* of the rifle the way I guessed Artie was waiting, shaping prayers with his lips, hunched behind the steering wheel waiting for the first bullet to shatter the rear window of the cab and smash into his skull. Except this time there was no *crack!* and no bullet and all his life Artie would remember they'd let him go, let him drive away with his miserable life like a dog crawling with its tail between its legs.

And Dog-girl was where she'd been summoned by

Enoch Skaggs, home on the Dundee Road where she belonged.

"What the hell?"—there was Vesta slow as a sleep-walker coming out of the kitchen to see what the commotion was. Her moon eyes glazed over and fleshy soft lips open, swollen breasts showing through a man's T-shirt and her belly so big—Vesta was seven months pregnant, proudly bearing Enoch Skaggs' seed—stretching her black nylon pants like a little barrel was stuffed inside. Her no-color hair was coming out in handfuls and her skin mottled and sore. Poor Vesta who'd been better looking than Dog-girl not so long ago. After Rhodena, Vesta was Enoch Skaggs' favorite. Seeing me but her eyes didn't take me in. Making her way barefoot across the floor cluttered with butts, beer cans, tossed-down clothes to come stand beside me panting, balancing the bulk of her belly by settling her weight back on her heels. A glisten to her skin, a twitchy smile. First time I'd set eyes on Vesta she was riding with Enoch Skaggs on his motorcycle, her arms clasped tight across the man's muscular chest, the two of them in hand-tooled leather vests and jeans and wearing shiny black crash helmets and silver reflector sunglasses so you couldn't see their eyes, whether they were looking at you or not. First time I'd set eyes on Vesta with him it was like with Rhodena I was weak with yearning wanting to be her, wanting to be any woman so prized by such a man.

Vesta wasn't young, maybe thirty. With the way sometimes of an even older woman carrying herself with caution lest she make some terrible error.

The stranger in the pickup was gone and the dog's barking was lessening and no one had been shot and Vesta turned to me with eyes widened in relief, her lips moved as if to identify me: "In-grid."

Enoch asked did I have the check? I fumbled to find it in my bag, my paycheck from Chautauqua County for two weeks, after taxes only two hundred sixty dollars eleven cents. Enoch cursed taking the paper from my fingers and smoothing it on the kitchen table. It was wrinkled, and somehow damp so the ink was smeared. "Come on. Sign your name." He'd turned the check over for me to endorse. I was holding a ballpoint pen but my fingers were shaky, I hate it when somebody watches me write like when I was in school at the blackboard and the teacher would say now watch Ingrid, she knows how. So I signed *Ingrid Boone* on one line and on the next wrote *payable to D. W. Nathan* which was one of the names Enoch Skaggs used. *D. W. Nathan* who had an account at the First Bank of Port Oriskany and could get his checks cashed there with no suspicion.

After his death they would say in the newspapers and on TV how Enoch Skaggs stole from us. His disciples who adored him. They would say it was the women and girls mostly who gave him money, since he'd been just a young kid, fifteen years old, in Keene Valley in the Adirondacks with girlfriends so crazy for him they obeyed his instructions going with men for hire. They would say he exploited and abused us but it could not have been so, tears of happiness and relief flooded my eyes when Enoch Skaggs told me to sign

my name, when he took the check from me and put it
into his wallet and drew his thumb rough and caress-
ing across my temple.

Dog-girl, home where you belong.

Each in turn they greeted me. Flatfoot, Zed, Bone,
Hammer. Vesta, Rhodena, Carlene. And others. (And
where was Gem?—I did not ask, not needing to know.
For what I needed to know I would be told at the
required time.) None of them were surprised that
Dog-girl had returned. It was supposed that Enoch
Skaggs had summoned me with his mind. His thoughts
cast like an invisible net of steel over how many miles
with the power to bring us to him whether or not we
wish to return. As Carlene spoke of Enoch Skaggs
summoning her from what she had believed to be a
hiding place hundreds of miles away with relatives.

From the excitement in their faces I understood that
something was to happen that night. I wondered sick
with dread and eagerness *Is it Dog-girl? The sacrifice?*

For somehow I had known about the *place of
bones* without being told. Sinking into sleep and in my
sleep entering the dreams of my family, my sisters and
brothers of Satan's Children.

I had known, I had always known. Even before
Enoch Skaggs was my husband I had known.

For always it had been whispered that Satan's Children were bonded by something deeper than just
word-vows and tattoos and what the eye could dis-
cern. The biker gang, Enoch Skaggs and his brothers
and his women—the sign of the X. They were like, yet
unlike, other biker gangs. Out of Buffalo, Port Oriskany, Yewville. Their Harley-Davidsons polished and

gleaming like jewels. Their leather gear, gloves, gold chains and gold ear studs. The drugs they traded in, and the drugs they took. A rumor of a young rich girl from Buffalo who'd ridden away with one of the men to live with Satan's Children and was never heard of again. A rumor of a family member, a guy suspected of being a police informant who was made to OD on heroin and his corpse delivered to the rear of the Port Oriskany police headquarters, dumped there by night. And the white suburban kids on their shiny Yamahas cruising Route 33 out of Port Oriskany along the lake or hanging out at Olcott Beach weekends and meeting up with Satan's Children, getting their heads cracked. A rumor that Enoch Skaggs had been sworn into the Aryan Brotherhood in the state prison at Red Bank where, aged nineteen, he'd been sent for seven years, for armed robbery and assault in Port Oriskany. And that a man had to kill a black man to be made a full blood brother.

A rumor that Satan himself was Enoch Skaggs' father and that his mother had died in agony, her body ripped apart giving birth to him.

"My allegiance is to Satan only."

Not to God, nor certainly to man. Even the German Nazis he admired, a black swastika entwined with a bright green snake tattooed on his left upper arm, hadn't their glory come to naught? Enoch Skaggs did believe in *race pride* as he called it. Prophesied that someday he would take his rightful place as *the scourge of the Aryan race of North America.* But that time was not yet. Now, there was Satan's Children which was the family of blood brothers and females under his leadership, all dependent upon him. And Satan his sire.

Did I believe? Yes, I would say I believed. I would say I did not doubt. Where there is such fear and such love as I felt for Enoch Skaggs there can never be a doubt.

To doubt, you must be strong. To doubt, you must have the power to be in two places at once in your mind. When I was Dog-girl of Satan's Children all my strength was required for me to be in a single place at a single time.

My mother, I had lost contact with. I never thought of her. I didn't know where she was living. Had she gotten married again. Had she ever gotten divorced from my father. If my father was alive, or dead. A rumor had come to us he was dead. An airplane crash in the Gulf of Mexico, the bodies of the pilot and passengers devoured by sharks. I never thought of it.

Of Enoch Skaggs' women who adored him Dog-girl was his favorite sometimes for a day or two, a single night. But never was I to be one of Enoch Skaggs' *wives*. There were those who were his *wives* exclusively and none of the other men dared touch them. Rhodena, Vesta, Carlene were Enoch's *wives*, for a while a girl named Arlina who was to disappear, and another whose name I've forgotten, and for these I nursed a savage hatred in my heart. Others of us, girls and women who came and went and were of a lesser value, were shared by the brothers and by Enoch when he wanted. Sometimes we were treated well, and sometimes not. There is this hunger in us that someone must feed. *Take of my heart and eat, and of my blood and drink.*

Enoch Skaggs named me *Dog-girl.* For my doggy-brown, shiny-brown eyes so needful. So hopeful. For my shivering when touched. For the love welling in me so eager to be spilled. All of my past Enoch said must be erased. All of my ties, memories. He laughed at me but it was the laughter of fondness, I believed. His weakness for me. For there was that side to Enoch Skaggs, as to most men, that weakness that shamed him. My long pale blond hair fine as cornsilk when I was able to keep it clean and shining and free of snarls. My face was a delicate doll's face, even the tiny nicks and scars in my eyebrows and high on my forehead were like flaws in porcelain. As if someone for some mysterious purpose had taken a scalpel to this face to mark it. And my thin body, beneath my clothes. Scars, scabs, the tracery of old welts never fully healed. Men love girls with blackened eyes and often my eyes were bruised, blackened. And needle tracks on the insides of my forearms like tiny bloodsucker mouths along the sunken blue veins.

Satan's Children knew only of Dog-girl that she was meek, yearning and in love with Enoch Skaggs. No one knew of the fires of lust raging in her heart.

Enoch Skaggs warned me with a smile baring tobacco-stained teeth *I am the bearer of precious seed, this seed must not be spilled or lost.*

Every woman and girl he fucked, he would wish to bear his child.

For the child would be a boy, he believed. A boy in his likeness and in the likeness of Satan who was Enoch Skaggs' true sire.

So Enoch Skaggs warned me with no subterfuge

that first time. So Enoch Skaggs pronounced the truth to me, bringing me to the farmhouse on the Dundee Road. Where I'd gone with him fearless, laughing. I'd gone with him drunk and laughing at the way the sky tilted like a bowl, the pavement flew beneath the Harley-Davidson's speed. Laughing and hugging a guy I didn't know, his chest in his leather jacket so wide I could hardly get my arms around it and that was funny, too.

That first time. That day, that calendar date I have tried to remember and cannot. They demand for you to be specific about dates for if you testify one thing at one time then forget or remember differently at another they believe you are lying, they will call you *perjurer.* Or *mentally incompetent—substance abuser.* So I was not able to provide specific dates because even if I seem to remember in my dreams it is only what I believe I remember and not any true fact. But it was a fall day two years ago, October probably—the leaves had turned overnight, bright slashes of sumac red, the yellow birch leaves, and willow—and the wind was cold. I didn't have any gloves, and my head was bare and hair whipping like crazy and I was drunk enough not to know where I was being taken, and who it was taking me, and not to ask questions. My life like dice I could toss, and toss, and toss to see what would happen.

I'd walked out on an older guy, an insurance salesman he called himself. A drinker, too. I loved him but he wasn't strong enough to keep me from going with other guys, practically in his face, where there's no respect there's no love. I'd stolen from him, too. Not just cash but clothes of his, expensive Italian boots he'd been boasting of I gave to another guy for the hell of it. And word got back to him, and maybe I'd be in serious trouble but I didn't care. There was too much going on, every night in whatever bar or tavern I turned up there was too much going on so I was feeling good, and I was looking good. My long hair shining around my face and my smile like an angel-smile if you didn't see the little scars and nicks in my face and there was Enoch Skaggs removing his dark glasses in the bar to look at me.

In that instant, Satan making his choice.

In that instant, never to be undone.

Climbing then up behind him on his Harley-Davidson, gleaming black and chrome, the motor vibrating, shuddering. The noise of it ripping the night. Clutching at this unshaven long-haired man with studs in his ears, snaky tattoos visible at his wrists, my thin arms tight around him as I could manage like I'd seen girls clutching their men, biker men, in envy. That motorcycle!—the sheepskin saddle, the roaring that set my teeth on edge, a wild jarring ride like nothing I had known before.

The roads were lined with trees. Flame-colored leaves like we were plunging through fire. Across the wire-humming metal bridge above the railroad yard, the Chautauqua River I'd been seeing all my life except I didn't recognize it then. Shimmering with fire, the sun breaking on the choppy surface. And the sky so open above like a canyon of such vastness the eye would never find rest.

Wasn't dressed warm enough for the wind. Wind tearing at my eyes, whipping my hair. Wearing just a nylon sweater over a shirt, and my jeans. What I wasn't prepared for was: how wide my legs had to stretch, to fit myself behind Enoch Skaggs who was a big man, my pelvic bones aching like they'd been pried open, my cunt open and gaping raw inside my clothes. One of our last times together she'd been drunk saying *Don't open yourself to any man, don't make that mistake like I did so young.* But Momma'd never set eyes on Enoch Skaggs.

Sped through the neighborhood set on a hill above the river, the cardboard houses, spindly trees and cracked sidewalks, the roar of Enoch Skaggs' motorcycle lifting behind us like a bright flaring banner. Along Route 11 and into the country, into farmland and open fields and the steep glacier hills. The Yewville creek, the railroad crossing at Post Road and Dundee Road, the old cider mill part collapsed above the creek—these sights rushed past my eyes that were blurred with tears. Speeding on a motorcycle it's an open cockpit, not like an enclosed airplane, there's nothing to protect you if the cycle bucks you off, if the seatbelt fails, if you lose the strength in your arms and knees gripping the driver you're gone, the rushing pavement so close, wind like steep walls of a canyon rushing past on both sides that's how close Death is! But I wasn't thinking such things. You never think such things. There came the old farmhouse back the lane, the weedy rutted-puddled lane we jolted along, could I identify any of this later I don't know. Not all things that happen to us are known by us. Where I was, wasn't a priority. Say you're a drunk eighteen-year-old girl going to be fucked by a biker-stranger you'd never seen before that night, the actual place like the actual time is not relevant.

In that house in a back room dim as a cave from vines grown over the windows Enoch Skaggs made his statement he was the bearer of precious seed. He was not an ordinary man. Not a mortal who would live and die like any ordinary man. He'd had certain signs he said. From birth onward. The flaming X tattooed on his chest was an outward manifestation of this destiny he said. Gold studs in his ears and the many rings he wore on both hands. *Satan begat me* Enoch Skaggs said grinning at me, my dazed scared look, pulling off my clothes till I stood naked before him, and opening his pants he wouldn't trouble to remove till later. *Satan is my father and all my power is from Satan, dumb cunt you don't believe, eh? don't get it, eh? You will.* Enoch Skaggs' winey-dark, ropey-veined cock lifting quivering from his dark groin was the sacred vessel bearing such seed, I would worship it, all women worshipped it, he grabbed my head lowering it by force to his cock so my tight-shut lips were pressed against it, I was kissing it, kissing him, shutting my eyes and kissing him as he bade me, the tip of the cock rubbery and moist exuding a sticky teardrop. Thick as my wrist was Enoch Skaggs' cock, blood engorged and alive giving off a humid radiant heat. Never kissed any guy like this before, never once sucked off any guy before, the disgust of it, the shame. But now no turning back, I started to choke when Enoch gripped my head tighter and tighter jamming his cock into my mouth, too weak to fight him off, his steely fingers ready to snap my neck like he could snap a cat's neck, he was out of control making a high whimpering keening sound, pumping himself into me like he wanted to kill me. Slipped out of my body observing from a

corner of the ceiling. Like Momma once said, I'd forgotten till now, she'd slipped from her body to
observe her baby girl being born. I saw a naked blond
girl skinny assed, bruised breasts no larger than pears,
ribs showing through her skin—was she anyone I
knew, anyone I gave a shit for whether she lived or
died? I was disgusted by her, I hated her—her silly doll
head gripped in a man's big hands and he's pumping
pumping pumping himself into her mouth, her mouth
pried open so her face is near to splitting, she's
choking, gagging, another few seconds and she'll pass
out and when she does he'll keep on till he's finished,
he'd fuck a dead girl and never take notice. This
sinewy-muscled man with the long straggly dead-black
hair, his face like something carved, eyes narrowed to
slits, gold studs glittering in his ears and gold chains
around his neck, flame-bright tattooed on his chest—
the sign of Satan. When he starts to come his eyes
open wide in astonishment and disbelief, his hips jerk
convulsively, he comes and comes whimpering like a
baby, weak-kneed now and staggering.

The girl gags, chokes, swallows—hasn't any choice,
he's mashing her head against his groin, still con-
vulsing. *I am the bearer of precious seed, this seed
must not be spilled or lost.*

That first time. Left me where I fell. Came back later
and wordless spread open my legs, fucked me, sweat
shining on his face like a bronze mask. His mouth was
twisted, his forehead creased with the effort. His cock
so big—hurtful—like he'd jammed his fist in me to the
elbow. I was crying, trying to scream and he pressed
the flat of his hand against my mouth, so heavy on me
I couldn't breathe riding me so my backbone splin-

tered. Beneath us was a flat hard mattress, sticky smelly sheets. Overhead a ceiling stained with rainwater the shade of dried pee. Jungle vines grown over the windows so only a greeny undersea light came through. Stabs of pain shot through me, my insides tearing, the more I struggled the more Enoch Skaggs liked it, grunting, laughing, finally seizing my hips and slinging my legs over his shoulders so he could pump himself deeper into me, deeper, harder, angrier until at last it ended—like he'd been shot in the heart, it was over. He collapsed wheezing and panting on me, gone limp. The two of us fallen from a great height not knowing if we were dead or alive. Or if there was any difference. I was crying, my arms around his neck. Fingers in the man's hair that was coarse as a horse's mane.

He'd made me bleed, he said a woman who can't bleed between the legs is a whore. Laid his hand on my cheek, stared at me. Like he was seeing me for the first time. His bleached-blue eyes, his hard-boned face. A briny sweat-stink lifting off him.

"Dog-girl, that's who you are. Doggy-eyes. *Nice.*"

By this time it was dark. The others were back and loud in the house. Enoch pulled on his pants and went out and I heard him say yeah she's ready. The first guy who came in, might've been Flatfoot. Or Bing. Or Gem. I lost track. Didn't know their names yet anyway.

Now he was calling, teasing—"Dog-girl, down! Down, down!"

Enoch Skaggs in one of his high-flying moods. He'd loved it scaring the shit out of Artie and everybody laughing at the spectacle. Smoking hashish now out of a pipe Carlene fixed for him.

They'd been whispering, grinning among themselves. Like some secret was about to be revealed. Glancing at me, Dog-girl, kind of excited and sly. Because I was so young or looked young, because I retained still the capacity to be surprised.

Enoch opened the cellar door, it was a flat door with a rusted iron ring, and took hold of me by the back of the neck like you'd grab a dog, not to hurt, just to guide, and pushed me ahead of him down the cellar steps that swayed under our weight. Into the dark earthy damp. Shining a flashlight but the battery was dying, faint light like fraying thread. Behind us Vesta was giggling. When the family'd first moved into the house they stored certain of their supplies in the cellar—guns, ammo, drugs, stolen items—but the stone walls leaked, the floor turned to mud and swill after a hard rain. Now they tossed garbage and trash down there when it was raining too hard or too cold and windy to go outside and dump it beyond the barns. The stink of rotting garbage was strong.

In a corner of the cellar there was a mound of trash, Enoch directed me to it gripping me by the shoulder and gave it a prod with his booted foot and it turned out to be a living person, Gem—"Hey shitface, you got a visitor."

Gem rolled over, blinking in the light from the flashlight and working his bloodied mouth. His face was swollen and boiled looking like meat and stippled with insect bites. He was barefoot, and his ankles and wrists were bound with greasy chains like bicycle chains and his right eye was the color of a rotted plum but when he squinted up at me where I stood a lewd light came into his face, I crossed my arms quickly over my breasts fearing I was naked.

I was naked and would be given to this man doomed to die. The two of us blood sacrificed to Satan.

Now I know Gem's true name, his baptismal name. The name that would be in the papers and on TV and pronounced in court. His age and where he was born. Then I did not know his true name, probably I believed his name was just Gem. The spelling of it I would have guessed—G E M.

Gem was Enoch's right-hand lieutenant. Or had been. As tall as Enoch and heavier in the gut, with a scarred forehead from a bike accident. He'd been crazy for motorcycles since he was a kid, had a weakness for stealing them, even a state trooper's cycle once, breaking them down for parts. He was from St. Lawrence near the Canadian border. Enoch's age, in his early thirties. They'd met at Red Bank, blood brothers in the Aryan Brotherhood. Gem's hair was carroty red, darkened and stiff with oil. His eyebrows were a lighter red and looked like they were lifting off his face. Drunk on beer or on uppers Gem was loud, unpredictable. He had crying jags. He stuffed his face eating till he puked. He saw people in the woods, out in the fields, training binoculars on him. Videotaping him. He believed the F.B.I. and the black race were conspiring to take over the U.S. He carried a gun, a fish-gutting knife stained with blood. I stayed away from him, out of the reach of his fingers that liked to snag in my hair, looping it around his fist. Out of the reach of his big booted foot. Gem was adoring of Rho-

dena who only laughed at him like you'd laugh at a
full grown shepherd dog craven before you. Saying sure
Gem's psycho but if psycho's on your side, that's cool.

Now doom was upon him, I could smell of the sad
stink of where Gem had pissed himself. He was covered in grime and cobwebs and his face so bloodied
and swollen but in the thin light from Enoch's flashlight he looked like a boy almost, somebody I'd sat
near in junior high in one of the schools Momma'd
enrolled me, blinking fast and eager and hopeful.

Enoch nudged Gem again with his foot. Saying,
"Here she is, Dog-girl. Come to pay her final respects."

I knew now: one by one the family had been
coming down into the cellar to pay final respects to
Gem. And Dog-girl the last, which was why I had been
summoned.

Gem squinted one side of his face like he was
having trouble hearing Enoch's words. A fat-bellied
little spider like a dust ball was making its way through
his hair, raising its legs so delicate and precise I
slipped into a quick dream of seeing Ingrid Boone just
a little girl walking through deep snow. Where we'd
lived in Tintern Falls, just Momma and me.

Gem worked his bruised mouth, pleading. "Hey
man, I'm not ready. I need more time, man. Hey"—

Enoch cursed and spat into Gem's face. "You had
all your fucking life to get ready, asshole. Nobody gets
a second chance."

Gem lifted his hands, his chained wrists, to appeal
to Enoch but Enoch would not listen. You could see
that Gem didn't believe what this was, what was happening to him, for always there might be a way of
turning it all around. For Enoch Skaggs was a person

of sudden reversals and surprises. But they were of his domain solely, no one else had access.

I was sick with fear of being left alone with Gem in the dark of the cellar but I knew it would be. More than once Dog-girl had been banished to the cellar, being willful in opposition to something I'd been ordered to do or failing to do it fast enough or doing it wrong, you could incur the wrath of certain brothers by just being in a place at the wrong time. Or by a look on your face, a crying look, you didn't know of. Like after Dog-girl fucked up in the Falls Shopping Center I was punched and kicked and pushed down into the cellar and quarantined as Enoch called it, maybe they forgot me away in Buffalo for five days and the cellar door weighted down with a heavy table. I would have starved except for garbage, would have died of thirst except for water trickling down the stone walls so cold and fresh to my tongue. Lying on the topmost steps my nose and mouth pressed to the crack of the door to breathe, slipped into my twilight state not-there and finally not-hungry a day and a night and a day and a night—you lose track, you float where Time is one single stream like Death, there's dignity in such knowledge. Momma said *A woman has to have her pride, without pride we're all animals.* But I was an animal, that was how I survived. And the look in Enoch Skaggs' face when he lifted the door, saw me lying there where he'd forgotten me, Dog-girl with her fingernails broken and bloody from clawing at the door. Saw me weak and helpless and my face hardly a face he knew but my eyes holding no more reproach for him than a baby lifting to his all love, adoration, gratitude for him returning to me and he squatted down and pulled me up into his arms like I was his bride.

Seeing into my soul deeper than any of you.

Saying, "I'm here to tell you, Dog-girl—your punishment has been just."

There was this unexpected kindness then. Which is what I meant about Enoch Skaggs. Lighting a joint to give to me and instructed me to minister unto Gem who had entered the valley of the shadow. Gem was a piece of shit who'd betrayed Satan's Children in some way I did not then comprehend but had no doubt it was so, now there was no turning back but, I was Gem's angel of mercy Enoch said.

Angel of mercy! My disgust of the cellar stink, my terror of the cave vanished. For I saw myself in that instant as Enoch Skaggs named me: *Angel of mercy.*

Enoch left me the flashlight too. Held it in one hand training the feeble light on Gem's chest where his shirt was ripped part open, bloody, scabby chest hair poking out like animal fur. With my other hand I raised the joint to Gem's blubbery lips—I saw how delicate-boned my hand was, the wrist small as a child's—so he could suck in the precious smoke greedy and anxious like a drowning man sucking at oxygen. There was this intimacy between us. There was this sacred time of how many minutes, or hours. Gem inhaled the smoke in deep shuddering breaths and his eyelids quivered in gratitude, he swallowed the smoke, choked and coughed and fell to sobbing then laughing rubbing at his hurt face with manacled hands so it started to bleed and he was more a man on speed than dope talk talk talk! telling me how he'd been a lost soul wandering the earth from the beginning of Time, he'd been to the deepest regions of Hell and he knew there *was* Satan but he was not ready to die. He wept saying he wanted to see his mother again, he had been a bad son to her. He had caused his father's death he believed and wanted to make amends. And there was a child, a little girl who was his daughter he was certain, he wanted to see her and make amends with the mother if the mother was still alive. Saying then, begging, "You could save me if you wanted to, Ingrid!—you could run away from here to somebody's house—call the police—Ingrid?— you hear what I'm saying?" surprising me he knew my name, never had I heard *Ingrid* on any of the men's lips, I wasn't sure how I liked it.

Gem talked, talked, begged, till the joint was burnt down to nothing. I hadn't taken a single hit I'd saved it all for Gem the doomed man.

Angel of mercy. That was a new thought. A new way of naming Dog-girl that had never been uttered until that hour.

A long time ago glaciers covered this part of the earth. Ice-mountains shifting and cracking and gouging out the earth. I have dreamt of them, I've seen the blue ice, hid my face against the terrible prongs of light that can pierce your eyes and your brain in an instant. After the glaciers melted the land left behind was a crazed place, such steep hills and fissures and shapes in rock predicting what history would bring. Even this cow pasture out behind the hay barn, the way it slopes downhill then drops to a creek filled with trash. And the moon rising through the trees.

They had to carry Gem up out of the cellar kicking and screaming he wasn't ready, begged Enoch to forgive him he'd never cross him again.

That night was a night of the three-quarter moon. Bright as any full moon. Enoch had waited for this special time designated by Satan for blood atonement. The sky like dark rushing water, thin strips of cloud blown across the face of the moon in a ceaseless stream. It looked like somebody was peeking at you through his fingers then taking the fingers away, glaring bright. The moon was Satan's and you could feel Satan's presence. Fell into a dream my eyes lifted upward and my neck craning and my soft mouth opened like a baby's. I knew I had been here before in this place marked by rocks and boulders dragged out of the fields into Satan's sign X and whatever was to happen, had already happened. Yet I could not remember it, my soul was untouched.

Satan's Children worshipped the moon, and the moons of a planet called Jupiter. Tattooed in pearly, shiny ink across Enoch's wide shoulders.

This was the place of sacrifice, the burial place it was called. There was already dug into the earth a shallow grave at the north pole of the X, dirt and stones heaped beside it. And Dog-girl's hands aching, the soft skin blistered from the splintery shovel handle.

Gem was dropped in the open grassy space by the grave. You saw sweat shining on his face. In rivulets down his face. Babbling and chattering, laughing, sobbing, arguing and interrupting himself, craning his neck to see us, calling us by name and each name drawn out and moanful as a prayer. In the moonlight in his black clothes, his black vest open showing gold-glinting chains, his legs spread Enoch stood with the machete uttering prayers to Satan in a high wailing voice like no voice I had ever heard before. And his words I could not comprehend, words of a language unknown to me—like a strange bird's cries, terrible and beautiful. A humming rose from Satan's Children, I was among them, I saw Gem forced to his knees and Enoch tore open his shirt and I saw the gleam of the machete in its rising and dipping, its slow ceremonial flourishes, the machete was one of the weapons I had never seen before, by moonlight I saw but afterward forgot, forgetting even as I was a witness, casting my eyes upward till they ached in their sockets *I am not-here, I am not-here.* Seeing the dark quarter of the moon that's visible all the time if you have the eyes to see.

That *pulsing pulsing pulsing* that's the moon's beat. The bright stony face seeing all and judging nothing.

Enoch was chanting, "Satan hear me—Satan guide my hand—SATAN SATAN SATAN"—rocking from side to side, glassy eyed, raising and dipping the machete, teasing like a cock pushing in then withdrawing pushing in then withdrawing each time a little deeper a little harder, Gem knelt shackled and paralyzed, just his mouth working in silence staring at the machete as Enoch raised it higher, higher crying—"I AM SATAN AND I AM HERE TO DO SATAN'S BUSINESS"—and swinging the machete so it was a streak of flame striking Gem's thick neck with such force his head almost flew from his body in a spout of black blood.

I didn't see but I knew. I wasn't watching, I was not

a witness but my eyes were staring, I could not look away. A cry went up from Satan's Children, from Dog-girl among them, a single astonished cry like coming, violent wild rush convulsive like coming you can't stop, can't stop can't stop.

Gem fell, Gem was a body in the grass. Twitching like a chicken with its head severed. A hog I'd seen butchered once, hanging upside down above a tub and its throat cut and so much blood, streams, torrents of blood, the hog squealing and writhing, eyes with sight in them that dimmed slowly. How long it's asked of you to die, a very long time it must be. Beat by beat, the heart pumping its agony. Jesus Christ would not be so cruel as Satan but Satan is the one who, when you call, he comes.

With his booted foot Enoch turned Gem onto his back. Blood gushing from Gem so it looked as if he was still alive, the blood was something he was trying to say. Enoch cried in a high jubilant voice, "SATAN. SATAN. SATAN." Hacked open Gem's chest, cutting out Gem's heart, lifting it high in the moonlight crying, "SATAN BIDS: TAKE OF MY HEART AND DRINK OF MY BLOOD"—and the family crowded in like starving beasts and one by one drank of Gem's heart's blood, some held the heart which seemed still a living pulsing thing in their hands and drank in frenzied rapture and others were fearful of holding it but brought their mouths to it as Enoch held it in both his hands, there came Dog-girl yanked to her feet fainting and acid-puke leaking down the sides of her mouth as one of the guys grabbed her beneath the arms, hands in her armpits walking her as you might walk a recalcitrant child or a rag doll, the others' hard jeering hands on her pushing her, "Dog-girl! Dog-girl!" even the women pushing her, and Enoch bared his teeth laughing gripping her by the nape of the neck and shoving the heart into her face smeared in blood, against her opened mouth, as Satan's presence filled the moonlit grassy space amid the rocks in their mysterious formation comprehended only from above—X.

I wasn't sorry Gem was dead. When he fucked me, he hurt me. His crotch stank worse than his feet.

You won't believe me if I say: Enoch Skaggs was meant to be a great man. A man of our century. He was meant to be famous. If any man ever communicated with Satan and knew Satan's power in his mortal being it was Enoch Skaggs.

When I was Dog-girl of Satan's Children I knew a truth vanished from my life now. Now I know truths, new truths are uttered to me every day like the names, numerals in a telephone directory, so many. But then I knew a single truth and that truth was my life.

It's the men who treat you like shit you're crazy for. For only they can tell you your punishment is just.

This is not the testimony I would give to the police, and at the trial. This is the secret testimony only you may know.

The Bones

The X tattooed into Dog-girl's sunken stomach was slow to heal.

Each prong of the X measuring four inches.

Lay still and you won't feel it. No pain.

Was it punishment, or love. Dosed with 'ludes and strapped down on the wooden table. Enoch Skaggs wielded his glittering knife careful as a scalpel. *There is no pain.*

Might have eviscerated Dog-girl the way you'd gut a chicken, with a turn of the wrist, a flashing blade. That was in his power.

Blood streamed in quick trickles out of the shallow wound, soaking into towels. Screaming inside the gag. Those eyes on me, Enoch Skaggs wielding his knife, I will never forget.

There is no pain, only the delusion of pain. Enoch Skaggs could lacerate his own flesh and not flinch, could lower his outstretched fingers into fire and not flinch. Just beads of sweat breaking out on his forehead, and his fingertips blistered and peeling afterward. Hoped to burn off his fucking fingertips, he'd said. Though Flatfoot seriously argued no, you can't— the prints just grow back, identical.

Never was it known if the procedure was a
success.

How many days then in bedclothes on the floor like
a cocoon, running a fever. The X leaking green pus.
One of the women saying, What if it's an infection?
You know what an infection is? Who's going to take
her to a doctor? One of the guys said, excited, What
doctor? Where?

I was crying to hear such kindness in that woman's
voice. The kindness you don't expect and don't
deserve, is what breaks your heart.

Wished, though, it was Rhodena and not Carlene
who cared for me. Rhodena the most beautiful of
Enoch Skaggs' wives, but sometimes cruel.

But it was Carlene bathing me, the throbbing
wound, in warm water, then in a liquid that stung.
Then taping a bandage over, made of a towel. Her
hands were icy-cold, skinny hands, trembling and tick-
lish. Her straggly hair falling onto my bare skin. I
threw my head on the rolled-up blanket, back and
forth gnawing at my lip, laughing. "Stop," Carlene said
sharply. "You're not a baby." Laying a wet cold cloth
across my forehead that burned, my eyes that were
popping out of my skull. "You'll look back, Ingrid,"
she said, "and you won't remember any hurt from his
hands. How you get to where you are, like me, you
won't remember."

The sharpness of her voice was a surprise. In my
fever I'd been seeing Momma there, worrying and
cursing over me. I'd been sent home from school, a
note from the teacher, Momma half lay beside me on
the bed murmuring over and over *What can I do!*

What can I do! There never was any answer to that question but just the passing of time.

The brothers of Satan's Children were gone. Ridden off on their motorcycles. There was a silence in this place as of waves parting. The starving dog had ceased his wild yipping and lay now at the apogee of his chain panting and drooling in the dust.

That time, or another time, when I was stronger, it was Carlene helping me to walk to the outhouse atop the hill. I'd been hearing angry men's voices but of course it was just the flies. Thousands and thousands of flies and yellow jackets, wasps. Afterward then taking me by slow steps our arms around each other's waist to show me the burial ground amid the giant rocks I had been thinking was a dream, part of my fever dream, and Gem not truly buried there, nor Dog-girl where she'd fallen and been dragged. Carlene was whispering to herself, or maybe to me, her eyes sly and secret behind a curtain of straggly hair. I would think it a sad cruelty, my sister Carlene would be burnt alive, or was she to be riddled with bullets, when the sheriff's men made their raid. One of the dead, the bodies taken from the charred and smouldering ruins *and Dog-girl her betrayer*.

But none of that was known then, nor suspected. How, turning back the clock's hands, you encounter only innocence, ignorance.

"Look," Carlene was saying, "—guess it's been some dogs, or something, digging." She wiped at her mouth. She pointed to some loose bones, grimy white and of the curved shape of rib bones, poking out of packed earth. And some grimy fabric like part of a blouse with machine-lace. A rock the size of a bowling ball, pocked with lichen, had been set at the head of this grave but it had rolled loose. Carlene said, "Which one of them that is, I don't know. It couldn't be Arlina, the bones wouldn't be picked clean so soon. It couldn't be Gem."

With her trembly hands she scooped up what earth there was, to try to cover the bones. You could see the paw marks in the ground. She was breathing hard, yanking out handfuls of grass, too. But whatever had been digging had dug out too many bones and I wasn't strong enough to help, bending over made me dizzy. I wasn't much help.

For many minutes then in that solitude amid rocks, thistly weeds, bones there were no words uttered between us. I count that time now as a sacred time. If somebody would have told me *One day you will betray even her, your sister Carlene* I could not have comprehended even the words.

Rhodena and Vesta and other women in the family were gone, I believe. Away with the men. It might have been Port Oriskany, and it might have been Buffalo. Carlene and I would look at each other, sallow-skinned and our eyes bloodshot, start to giggle, mash our fingers into our mouths to be still but bursting into peals of laughter anyway. In even that sacred place.

The sun was gone, a heavy rain came hissing and steaming. Loosing steam from the giant rocks like breaths. If Satan was in this place, he did not show his face, but there were certain signs. A low humming, booming. A voice from the underside of the earth. But no words I could comprehend. Such knowledge was not for Dog-girl, nor for Carlene her sister.

Walking back to the house slipping and sliding in the wet grass. Our arms around each other's waist feeling each other's thin curved bones. I said, "I'd love for there to be rain always!—everything so clean, smelling so clean."

"On the last day, Judgment Day," Carlene said, "—all the bones of the world will rise and float." She fell to coughing, and wiped her mouth. She said, "I used to know more about it, but I don't, not now."

Shy like knowing I shouldn't ask, but needing to, I said, "How can there be so many bones in the hill? You did some others, I guess?—before I came here?"

Carlene shrugged. Drew just a little bit away from me, I could feel her stiffening spine. "The earth is filled with bones," she said. "We only put such a few there."

In the
Earthen
Cellar

In the earthen cellar where invisible beetles crawled over Dog-girl's fevered face, burrowed into her sticky hair. In the humid darkness quivering like breath. In the night shading into day shading into night and again into day perceptible by advancing and retreating gradations of light against the vine-choked window hardly more than a slot in the darkness. The slow turning of day to night, night to day, like the turning of the Earth upon its axis which now I could feel, my bony back flat against the ground, liquid waste leaking hot, scalding from my body soaking into the earthen floor, my life leaking from me. *I love you! Help me!*

Close overhead there were heavy footsteps. Floorboards creaked. There were loud voices. Frequent laughter. Quarrels flaring up swift as wildfire, a chair's legs scraped across the floor. Something dropped, shattered. A door was slammed shut. There were men's voices, and women's. They had forgotten Dog-girl tossed into the darkness with the garbage left to decompose, rot into the soil. Or were they speaking of Dog-girl, obsessively of Dog-girl, of no one other than Dog-girl next to be sacrificed? In the burial ground, amid the giant stones? By moonlight? Dog-girl's still-beating heart torn from her body by Enoch Skaggs' skilled hand, lifted to Satan? *Take of my heart and drink of my blood* and if this was so I reasoned calmly that Enoch Skaggs would forgive me, and love me again as he had. For if they hurt you bad enough the evil runs through them like an electric shock and is gone.

The X tattooed into my stomach was alive now with pain. The X twin prongs of flame illuminating my flesh. I was waiting for Enoch Skaggs to remember me, to descend the stairs to me, to inspect his handi-work. How many times hearing his footsteps on the stairs, the unmistakable presence, the weight of him, the smell of him feeling his hand on my shoulder shaking me awake. That sudden laughing way of his, almost boyish, seeing how he'd scared you, a sudden relenting as of petting a dog instead of kicking it as it cringes in anticipation. *Dog-girl! Baby! What the hell are you doing down here?* Lifting me in his hard, strong arms like I'm no more than a child.

But Enoch Skaggs did not come, not even in a fever-dream did Enoch Skaggs come and sleeping and waking and sleeping in that cellar grateful to be devouring like a wild animal what garbage was tossed from the top of the stairs I knew he would not come, none of them except my sister Carlene at infrequent intervals descending with a flashlight cautious and muttering to herself her hands badly shaking bringing me water in a tin cup and doughy hot-dog buns with slices of cheese inside, or strips of meat I could not eat except chewing slowly, slowly swallowing gagging as if my throat was shut against nourishment and if I fell asleep in the midst of chewing reviving me swiftly and roughly wiping my scummy face and mouth with a towel and brushing my hair out of my eyes but saying nothing never uttering the name *Ingrid* nor even *Dog-girl* and if I clutched at her bony wrists my fingers were pushed away as of no more consequence than strands of cobweb. And there crouched in a corner of the cellar the girl from the shopping center, the plumpish girl with her hair tied back in a ponytail *Gail Ellen* or was it *Gayellen* my friend in school one of my closest friends regarding me with astonished eyes. Eyes of horror, and of hurt. Knowing herself betrayed for this time I called to her, I spoke softly and cajolingly to her and did not drive her away to save herself but helped to overpower her, helped the guys to grab her with their quick hard hands, lifting, dragging into the rear of the van, a hand over her mouth to muffle the screams, helping to bind wrists and ankles with the wire, the terrible wire cutting into her baby-soft skin I was crying *Damn dumb bitch! Cunt! This is what you deserve!* And then maybe they would forgive me? All of Satan's Children would forgive me? And love me again? For certain of the brothers had a weakness for me, that weakness of which Enoch Skaggs had come to be ashamed, staring at me as if their eyes moved involuntarily onto me, their fingers twitching, even Gem so crude and hurtful, and one of them called Pitman months ago, stroking my hair that was healthy then, not so thin and tattered saying how pretty I was, how much he liked me he didn't like to see me hurt and he'd stroke with his thumb my cheek, my bruised eye asking what my name was and where I was from and how old and how'd I happen to come to this place and telling me of his daddy who was a farmer in Milburn and how they didn't get along and he'd gone off and tried to join the Navy but they didn't want him and he'd come back on Halloween and set fire to his daddy's hay barn beginning to kiss me, run his callused fingers over me, and there was nobody close-by, nobody to hear if I called out for Enoch Skaggs, or not. And a weakness for scars, scabs. Picking off scabs. And a flashlight shone in my face waking me and blinding me and it was the one called Flatfoot drunk on beer crooning *Let's see how you're healing baby* shining the light on my stomach, whistling at what he saw prodding the scab, picking at it with his nails like a little boy might pick at his own scabs to draw blood *Hey! sorry* kneeling beside me, swaying his head crooning *You're making me hard, Dog-girl making me want to fuck you that's what you want, huh?* and I could not push him away, could not fight him grunting as he shoved it into me, or partway in, I was so dry there, shriveled like my breasts now almost flat against my rib cage, the nipples no more than goose bumps. And panting, grunting *Oh baby, baby, baby* until he came, how many minutes it required for him to come, pumping himself into me his scrawny weight upon me his breath reeking of beer, rotted teeth and the pain of it like fire and I was crying, trying to cry and Flatfoot said *There's nobody up there to hear you* his forearm pressed against my mouth, then it slipped and jammed against my throat and the flashlight where it had rolled shone a slanted light onto Flatfoot's face, his scruffy beard you could see growing out of his jaws, his chin weak like the bone had begun to melt away, his nose that had been broken in a motorcycle accident and hadn't mended right and the shiny scars on his forehead and his eyes glistening out of the dark, drunk and shamed, when a guy is shamed to himself you are most in danger knowing how quick shame turns to anger, rage, that need to inflict hurt further than they've already done, and irrevocably. So I believed that Flatfoot would kill me mumbling to himself staring at me or at what he saw to be me but instead he released the pressure on my neck, rising fumbling with his pants then stooping again to grope for the flashlight saying in a vague wondering voice like thinking aloud *My name wasn't always Flatfoot* but he didn't say what his name had been and when I opened my eyes again he was gone. Only the cold phlegmy cum on my thighs drying.

I was in a phone booth at the bus station in Port Oriskany and a wasp buzzing inside the booth so I couldn't hear my own words clearly, my own fucking words in my fucking head and she was interrupting *I can't hear you Ingrid, where are you?* and I said I didn't know saying I needed help, I needed money and she said *Ingrid? I can't hear you* and I was sobbing nudging my head against the inside of the booth and the buzzing was louder *God damn it honey speak up, I can't hear you, for Christ's sake Ingrid don't do this to me I don't need this are you still there? Ingrid?* and I was beginning to freak, the buzzing so loud I was panicked this was not a safe place as in a dream there are safe places and dangerous places and the one may resemble the other and confuse you and her voice now pleading, angry *Tell me where I can come to get you Ingrid, oh please don't hang up* rising to a scream as if she could see his hand moving to take the receiver from me.

* * *

Began to see Momma's face. And to hear her voice
muffled at first, in the distance. And the creaking floorboards close over my head, and her voice lifted
scolding and worried so faint I could almost not hear
Ingrid where are you? Ingrid honey the words fading
so my heart was close to bursting and I opened my
eyes seeing I was under the porch, not in this place I
did not know but under a porch hiding, I was not
Dog-girl but a child hiding from my mother hearing
her footsteps quick and light close above my head, I
could see through the rotted latticework of the porch
and a tangle of vines Momma's legs in white slacks,
the scissorslike movement of her legs and her slender
hands lifting to her hair in a gesture of bemused exas-
peration *Ingrid honey where are you? C'mon don't be
a bad girl you know your momma loves you, and
your daddy.*

The
Betrayal

This is how Enoch Skaggs died that morning: riddled with bullets as he ran from the flaming house, a shotgun in his hands in the very act of firing both barrels blind into the barrage of bullets striking no discernible target among the Chautauqua County sheriff's men, it may have been that a scream burst from him, a final outcry of fury, hatred, defiance or it may have been a scream of disbelief taking his death, he who should not have died, from faceless anonymous uniformed men, a voice amplified through a bullhorn, the swirling red lights of police cars parked along the rutted lane as in a vertiginous blur dozens of bullets tore through him so his blood and meat-tissue and certain of his organs and his intestines would seep out onto the grassless ground where he fell beside the rust-desiccated hulk of an abandoned tractor seeping like cooked fruit leaking through cheesecloth, that old country way of canning where you strain the soft shapeless fruit through the cloth *drip drip drip* this is how Enoch Skaggs died that morning in the yard of the farmhouse off the Dundee Road.

Starved to eighty-six pounds when they weighed me. Skin tight as a drum, and jaundiced. Covered in

insect bites, bruises and scabs and the festering X
tattoo on my stomach. Lost so much weight in those
days and nights of captivity (I would estimate afterward as about two weeks) I was able to push myself
through the slot of a window where you'd think a full-
grown cat could not have pushed itself. And in the
night there was no moon, Satan lacked eyes to
observe. And crouched over half-naked my filthy hair
in my face like an animal making my way through the
orchard of misshapen trees their leaves coldly fluttering crackling like paper in the windless dark and
through to an open field doubled over in pain crawling on my hands and knees how many minutes, how
many hours through a maze of wild rose and brambles
like jeering laughter and in a ditch of spiky brackish
weeds I was too weak to continue even to lift my head
I slept hoping to summon my strength I saw Momma
in the road I had not known was so close, only a few
yards away, Momma pacing smoking her cigarette
seeming unaware of my presence *Ingrid? Where are
you?* Momma's plaintive voice borne by the wind
Ingrid? Ingrid the sound fading and I could not lift my
head, I tried but could not, until at last the sky began
to define itself out of the darkness like coalescing
pieces of ice in freezing water and the sun appeared at
the tree line a faint drained red under reefs of red-
stained cloud and I heard the voice now distant, now
closer *Ingrid are you lost? Ingrid where are you?
Ingrid!* impatient and worried and I tried to reply but
had not enough strength, my throat tight as if the flesh
had grown over rendering me mute. *Momma don't
leave me! Momma wait* I begged in silence but she
was gone, there were headlights in my eyes out of

nowhere I'd crawled into the road and now a car
shuddering to a stop skidding in the gravel and there
was a car door opened and a man's voice *My God
what is it?* and a woman's voice in a cry of horror *It's a
child, it looks like a child.*

That was how Ingrid Boone was saved, and Satan's
Children betrayed.

Brought to Chautauqua Falls to the hospital and
after several days when I could speak coherently I told
the police about Enoch Skaggs and Satan's Children
and the sacrifice of Gem and the burial ground and
the bones and Dog-girl and the drugs they traded in
and all I could recall of the family's myriad cruelties
and even their random kindnesses enumerated with
care, the X tattooed on my stomach in scar tissue a
sign *that I had been chosen. For what destiny I had
thwarted, yet it had been my own.*

My voice was hoarse and cracked like a voice long
unused. Pride and shame in equal measure.

And what is your name? they asked, they asked
repeatedly, *who are you, where is your family, your
home?* and I looked away, I shut my eyes. Could not
utter that name. Could not involve my mother nor any
Boone relatives however distant and unknown to me,
could not bear the shame of it. *I'm not from this part
of the country* I said *I'm from Florida, lived in different places in southern Florida and only came
north last year. Crystal Lake* the name came to me as
out of a dream but vaguely recalled, *My last home was
Crystal Lake.*

All that I told the Chautauqua authorities about

Satan's Children, all that would constitute my sworn testimony, was the truth as I believed it. But a truth shredded and mangled like skeins of cloud blown across the moon. For what I can remember is but a fraction of what was, as all that *is* is but a fraction of what *was*.

The first examining doctor did not believe my age which was nineteen insisting I could not be more than fourteen. His face and the faces of the attending nurses suffused with horror, pity. Dog-girl so battered, bruised, scarred. Bones jutting. Ugly inflamed tattoo on her belly. Lacerated, infected vagina. Infected kidney. Hair falling out in handfuls. And the needle tracks, a dozen or more on the insides of my thin arms. *Junkie. That's her secret: no-name junkie.* Almost impossible to locate a vein for the IV fluid, finally found one in my right ankle. Strapped down for my own well-being, fed through the nose, fed Haldol for the cessation of bad visions. And my ragged nails cut short, and my hands encased in thin rubber gloves so I could not pick at my face. I was a special patient at Chautauqua General in a private room protected by a twenty-four-hour police watch. For fifteen days in that room, nourished by medicines I could not have named except to know *my new life is beginning! Dog-girl's destiny thwarted!* By the time of my release and transfer to the Chautauqua County Women's Detention Center the sheriff and his men had already staged their raid, all but three of Satan's Children, all men, had been killed, shot down by police or burnt alive in the farmhouse and this fact I seemed to know though I can't remember how I knew, if it was one of the nurses who befriended me who told, or the sheriff's

deputy outside my room, or a Chautauqua Falls newspaper smuggled in to me, or maybe I had dreamt it
squirming and thrashing in my bed—the swirling red
lights of the police cars in that early morning before
dawn, the amplified voice through the bullhorn, the
exchange of gunfire, the death of Enoch Skaggs as he
emerged from the burning house to fire a shotgun
into a barrage of bullets, the spear-flames leaping from
the tar-paper roof of the old house, the boiling roaring
flames in which Carlene and the others died, Vesta
who was eight months pregnant, eleven of them to die
that morning of the surprise raid, and Dog-girl among
them shrieking in terror.

My new life! My destiny thwarted.

The Shrine

Of the several towels soaked and stiffened with his blood she kept one, unable to bring herself to throw them all away. And she had an undershirt of his, a white T-shirt grimy at the neck and spotted too with blood, she'd never laundered. And there was a single necktie of the fewer than a half dozen he'd owned, a flat dull green in a fabric so synthetic it had no texture, no weave at all—where had something so ugly come from? Must have bought the tie himself, hurriedly, in a Woolworth, or Sears, or some dismal men's clothing store in one or another small town, for which of his consultations with authority, county prosecutor, district judge, hastily retained lawyer she could not recall, if she'd ever known.

And there were the Kodak snapshots. Precious, irreplaceable. You can't ever guess in the hilarity of the moment, somebody taking your picture, you're clowning for the camera arms around each other's waist holding beer cans, or kissing—can't ever guess what these snapshots will mean one day. The two of them just kids!—it makes her dizzy to see. How pretty she'd been, how sassy and arrogant and *him*—so good-looking, that crest of hair, that grin, just the way he stood—takes her breath away. She'd dropped out of high school to marry him. In this picture, she'd been already pregnant. But not showing. A secret. Crazy for each other, the two of them, *can't keep their hands off each other* as it's said. A sort of flame enveloping them. And there was a single snapshot of him in Vietnam, Navy uniform lounging in front of his jet bomber, hair shaved short, crease in his forehead and he's just turned from talking, laughing with some friends also in uniform, guys his own age, killer-kids, names unknown. Can tell it's a foreign country by just the humid look of the light. Strange misty radiance of the sky that seems to be no color at all.

What they'd done to him in Vietnam, in his soul, she'd never been able to comprehend, let alone modify. Or maybe he'd always been a killer in his soul like so many men she's known, and there he'd learned how once you kill it's only just something you've done on your way to doing something else like sleeping, or eating, drinking, or returning home, loving. Whatever you do, you do. Sometimes people manage to stop you because it's their job to stop you, but sometimes they don't, and that's all right, too. *Whoso sheddeth man's blood, by man shall his blood be shed; for man is made in the image of God.* And that's all right, too.

Pictures of them with a baby, which baby?—she knows it must be her daughter but the thought stabs, almost it's panic, the infant boy who'd died, Goddamn fuckers allowed him to die, doctor, hospital, insisting it was nobody's fault nobody's negligence born six weeks premature and the meningitis had ravaged him, nobody's fault but she knows better, she's always known. It's that anger, that rage and inexpressible hurt she's drinking down, sipping and savoring in her mouth before swallowing, the good burning sensation going down, then the numbness. But these pictures are of the little girl, the other pictures, of the boy, had been ripped up, lost years ago. The little girl raised aloft in her daddy's hands *Hey look this is mine! ours!* and she, the mother is beside them young-looking as a high school girl with the blond hair, sexy in a red halter top displaying her perfect breasts, cutoff jeans high on her lovely smooth thighs, and she's barefoot, toenails painted bright red to match her fingernails. The picture was snapped at the old Marsena airport that's closed down now, there's the Vultee behind them, big handsome tin-colored plane, Luke's favorite. Who might have been holding the camera?—probably Vaughn Brownlee. Dead for years. And the curly-haired child Ingrid kicking in her daddy's strong hands maybe two years old. Daddy, Momma and little Ingrid smiling into the future so happy because the future never seemed anything more pressing than just the next hour, or that evening at Wolf's Head Lake where they'd have supper at one of the outdoor tables.

You know I love you. Even if I can't always say it right. Or show it.

Not many snapshots of him, of the three of them. Things get mislaid, lost in moving. You're leading a confused life, a messed-up life she's been told. Things get lost. And maybe she'd ripped up snapshots herself, in a rage. Furious sobbing, a wish to *rip! rip! rip!* whatever she could get her hands on.

Later, you regret it. Sure. That's part of it: regret.

She had been able to find only that single snapshot

of Luke at an airport, Christ how he'd loved those planes, she'd been fearful of them herself, had to be a little drunk to fly with him without panicking and without him guessing her true feelings. So one day she scissors a photo of an Air Force jet bomber out of a newspaper, another day she gets hold of a dozen back issues of *Flying* and scissors out photos of planes that resemble the ones Luke flew, or might have flown. Eventually, over a period of months, she includes photos of pilots with their planes where the pilots' faces are indistinct. Knows it's a little strange, cutting out strangers' pictures, but it gives comfort, it's just for her, for the secret treasure as she thinks of it, in her bedroom, at first displayed on the top of her bureau then spilling over onto windowsills, bedside table. Just something she finds herself doing when she isn't doing something else. *What else is life except what you're doing when you aren't doing something else, and the next thing you do is that something else. And so what?* And, in time, she adds more photos, glossy pictures of, for instance, a fiery sunset in Key West she knows Luke would have seen many times, and a stark chill moonrise above the Grand Canyon she knows Luke would have liked to see, and a dazzling-crystalline ice floe in the Arctic he'd have liked to see, too—whistling thinly in that way of his *Jesus! is that beautiful.* And there was a map of Florida where she'd circled in red ink Crystal Lake which was about ninety miles west of Miami, and there was a map of the Caribbean, both maps much-folded and creased. (These were tacked to a wall.) And there was an empty Camels pack—not his, but in time she would come to think, to be certain, it had been his,

and anyway isn't it indistinguishable from any of the
hundreds of empty Camels packs he'd crumpled and
tossed aside in his life. And there was a battered but
still jaunty-looking russet-brown fedora she'd found
on a Greyhound bus, not Luke's of course nor had he
ever worn such a hat but if he had, Jesus how good-
looking how sexy he'd have looked. And there was a
gold watch, a Seiko, very attractive with a wide stretch
band, not Luke's either and in fact the lost or misplaced or purloined property of a man, a drinker,
who'd taken her out a few times, somehow there was
a strong connection between Luke and this watch.
*Sees him tearing the tinsel wrapping paper, opening
the little box and there's the watch and he's smiling
slipping it over his knuckles, onto his wrist and his
arm is around her shoulders and he's kissing her. It's
Christmas, she sees the snow-reflection through the
window, ghostly-glimmering onto the ceiling.* And
there was an antique-looking amethyst ring in fact
glass but very beautiful a man friend had given her but
Luke might have given her, and in time she'd come to
believe, to be certain, Luke had. And there were
candles, squat pastel incense-candles from a shop at
the mall, she'd sometimes light. And there was a bou-
quet of blue hydrangea artificial but so real-looking
you might be fooled into smelling them. And there
was a single playing card, a joker, stiff with grime
appropriated from what deck in which tavern or in
whose house she could not have recalled, the joker so
very masculine, sexy and treacherous with his gold-
spangled torso, his sly grin and yellow eyes slitted like
a cat's. *God's the joker, never know what He's going*

to do next, which trick He's going to play but you always know He's going to do something.

But maybe Luke is the joker, too. Or was. Maybe. If she thought hard about it. If, sipping her drink, turning the card in her fingers, brooding, smiling, shaking her head, wiping her eyes and tossing the card down as if it's a card she's playing she thinks long enough and hard enough about it which probably she won't, not right now.

Makes her choices by instinct. What she brings home to add to the secret treasure, the memorial.

The only absolute rule seems to be, this is nothing she has formulated but it seems to be so, she must never throw any of these sacred items out.

And one morning after she'd moved yet another time, in this new neighborhood at the edge of Mt. Ephraim she was walking along the silt-softened shore of the river after a night of pounding rain her heels sticking in the mud and she was wearing dark glasses because the air was bright and splotched reflecting off the water and it was windy which seemed to blow the brightness, the achy brightness straight at her, and there was a familiar river smell, river stink, something faintly sour, rotted but not unpleasant to her nostrils and she was trying to clear her head trying to accelerate the routine process of clearing away a hangover, it has much to do with moving *with* the pounding beat of your blood, moving *with* the pain not recoiling from it, and she was smoking a cigarette, the wind snatching at the smoke and blowing it away like gay, random, reckless gestures of the hands, she didn't remember lighting this cigarette nor even when she'd started smoking again for she'd quit, cold-turkey quit, a couple of years before and been Goddamned proud of herself, but now, somehow, she was smoking again but *Fuck it: why not?* Smoking helped sober her, helped sharpen her senses, steady her shaky fingers and she'd need steady fingers later that morning. At least when fitting the customer, when the customer could see. And if she started hemming the brides-maids' dresses as she'd better if she wanted to get them finished on time, lovely raw silk so delicate you can't be too careful with the needle, your touch light enough. So she was smoking and it was good for her and she was enjoying it, the way Luke had enjoyed it, teaching her to smoke as a kid, those deep lung-filling breaths, releasing smoke like a drawn-out sigh. And she was walking away from town in the direction of the Water Street bridge down behind the old Metho-dist cemetery, amid mud, litter, storm debris, car-casses of things so long dead they might never have possessed life, animation in any way resembling her own and it was a windy autumn day, late September and already many of the leaves blown from the trees and she was careful to think nothing to upset her, no thoughts of her daughter whom she'd last seen eight months before in circumstances she did not wish to recall and no thoughts of her husband whom she understood in moments of stark unsparing sobriety she would never see again nor even thoughts of the more immediate tasks of the upcoming day. Her mind was purposefully empty as the sky reflected choppily in the water. And it was in this state of being she saw, almost entirely covered in mud, a jar, or vase, of bright bitter-green glass, with a fluted rim, and her heart con-tracted in that quick hurtful yet not unpleasurable way that meant she'd discovered yet another item, yet another piece of the jigsaw puzzle to bring home with her. Squatting so that the calves of her legs ached, this was an unusual posture for her, and stretching her arm as she did, her grasping fingers reaching across a rippled span of mud to grab hold of the vase, tug at it and free it and hold it to the light: had his eyes been that color? There was some signal here, some sign she dared not miss. Washed the broken vase in the river, lifted it again to the light, breathing quickly now, excited, elated, her head ringing not so much with pain as with clarity, squinting at the glass, seeing the sky through the glass, that darkish-bright green, the color of his eyes, or the color his eyes should have been.

So Happy

"Come see me, Ingrid. Stay with me. For a few days. Or just overnight." My mother's voice over the phone was breathless, happy. Her words were clear and not slurred. "Next week is your birthday, isn't it? You owe me that, at least."

Now Satan was vanished from the world, many spaces had opened up. I would try to love my mother again, but not in the old way.

It was my twenty-first birthday. I would not have thought I could live so long. But it had happened.

That river! It's Mother's blood she can't escape.

She was calling herself Chloe McDiarmid now, living still in Mt. Ephraim though no longer on slummy Mohawk Street in a run-down duplex, now on Palisades Avenue in an old stone house of many windows, pale-pink limestone facade that glittered in the sun on a high snowy hill above the Chautauqua River.

The river was edged with ice like jagged teeth but dark and swift-running at its center. When I crossed it, on the Water Street bridge, wind rocked my borrowed compact car. I did not need to look down at the river to know that it was there.

Over the telephone my mother had been vague about where she was living now, and how long she'd been there. Who owned the house, whether she was living alone. I was surprised to see the size of the house. It was on a large wooded lot at the edge of Mt. Ephraim's "good" residential neighborhood but it was not in good repair and when my mother opened the door my vision was blotched for a moment and I thought *It isn't her, it has to be a stranger.* But my mother was already hugging me and calling me *Ingrid, honey* and I was hugging her in return so it was all right.

I'd brought Mother a present. A poinsettia plant, the petals a vivid dark red, leaves stiff and glossy. It was in a tinsel-wrapped earthen pot and was quite heavy and when Mother took it from me she laughed in her thin breathless way her breath sweet with liquor and ashy with cigarettes, kissed me again thanking me but saying it was my birthday wasn't it, I shouldn't have brought her anything.

She had something for me, a birthday present for me she said. She'd be giving me later.

The rooms of the pink limestone house were high-ceilinged and drafty and only a few of the downstairs rooms, which Mother took me through, were furnished. I recognized some old pieces of furniture set down in this strange space. Other pieces were new to me, but not new. Most of the windows had no curtains or drapes, nor even venetian blinds. Mother's high rapid chatter echoed above our heads.

She'd been worried about me, Mother said. Driving down from Chautauqua Falls by myself. Why hadn't I taken the bus? Why hadn't I called before I'd left? Did I know there was a traveler's advisory warning for all of Western New York?—a sleet storm was predicted overnight.

"Anyway, you're here. Thank God."

I was shy in Mother's presence. We had not seen each other in some time.

Mother was older, she was forty years old yet not much changed since I had last seen her, in the Chautauqua County courthouse at one of my hearings. I had asked her not to come, please stay away and not involve herself but of course she'd come, and she'd spoken to the judge, and made a good impression on him, and helped my case. Two years' probation, no prison sentence. Two years' psychiatric counseling. I knew my mother's presence would count in my favor but I had not wanted her to attend the hearing, I'd wanted to spare her and to spare myself. She was not much changed from that time but her hair was cut shorter, a stylish wave across her forehead, very blond, with a synthetic sheen. Her skin was drier and there were faint white lines around her eyes and a sadness in those eyes like water seeping into a hole you've dug in the earth but she was smiling, smiling and her mouth was a beautiful woman's mouth, mobile, accustomed to attention. Very red, glossy. And her cheeks rouged, expertly. And she was wearing good quality clothes, as if my visit was a special occasion. A fuzzy white angora *sweater set*, beige-and-white checked wool trousers. Like a woman in a fashion magazine. Sunburst gold earrings, several rings on her fingers. Lilac perfume dabbed behind her ears, on the inside of her elbow. When she hugged me as she'd done

several times, impulsive, girlish, I shut my eyes and
did not breathe and my heart ceased beating.

*Never told you, how you saved my life. Crawling
out of that hole.* There were not the right words to tell
such a thing. At least, to tell such a thing aloud, to
another person.

And her eyes on me, trailing over me. As we sat in
the kitchen talking. And her bright persistent smile.
Checking out my face which was her daughter's face
yet strange to her now. The faint scars in my forehead,
right eyebrow. Tiny sickle scar on my upper lip. There
were other scars, blemishes, discolorations hidden
inside my clothes that Mother could not see. Yet it
seemed she was staring at my body which was her
daughter's body through my clothes her eyes quivering with emotion even as her bright mouth moved.

How good it was to see me, how much she'd
missed me. How good I was looking. Yet there was a
question in her face, too. So finally I laughed, it was
a harsh unexpected laugh and I drew my sweater
sleeves to expose my arms, holding them out to show
Mother the insides of my arms where the needle tracks
were almost healed, invisible.

"Oh, Ingrid!"—Mother's voice was hurt, that I would
think she'd doubted me.

Now Flora Wells had died and her quality ladies'
clothing store was gone, Chloe McDiarmid had taken
on a number of her customers, sewing custom-made
clothes for well-to-do older women. She did fittings in
a room of the house, kept her sewing equipment
there, bolts of cloth, dressmaker's dummies. Spoke
proudly of her work with that seamstress's habit of

moving her fingertips lightly, suggestively as if the secret of sewing were contained in her fingers, a secret craft and a secret pleasure. I did not think that a seamstress's income in a city as small as Mt. Ephraim would be enough to support Mother, but I said nothing.

An hour into my visit a pickup truck turned into the driveway and parked behind my Camaro and a man Mother called Zach stomped in out of the snow, dropping by as if by chance. I saw that Zach was Mother's good friend, they were easygoing and mildly bantering together, Mother pouring whiskey for Zach, exchanging tender glances. Mother had told Zach that her daughter was coming to visit, this was the troubled daughter, the daughter who'd been in trouble, mixed up with the biker gang he'd surely have heard of, headlines shouting SATAN'S CHILDREN, RITUAL KILLINGS, ELEVEN DIE IN SHERIFF'S RAID, but the girl was all right now, was fine now, trying to live a normal life now so maybe Zach should drop by just to say hello. So Zach did. A heavyset man in his late fifties with mottled skin, large pores on his nose, a left eye that veered out of focus and a right eye shrewd as a marksman's. He wore a Merco Feeds cap clamped down on his head, a battered sheepskin jacket tossed familiarly onto a table by the kitchen door. His rubber boots were splashed with dried mud. Zach Houston, shaking my hand, owned a lumberyard in town, he'd lived in Mt. Ephraim all his life he said. Built like a steer, thick-necked. Quick loud laughter, crinkling eyes, the kind of man always in charge, knows exactly how much he should pay for what, cross him and you'll regret it. But Zach liked me, Chloe McDiarmid's grown-up daughter, or gave that impression. Liked to hear that I was attending classes at the college in Chautauqua Falls and working part-time in the registrar's office, supporting myself. I had finished my probation under the jurisdiction of the New York Department of Corrections and I had finished my two years of twice-weekly therapy at the Outpatients' Clinic of Chautauqua Falls General Hospital and I was free now of all drugs even the antidepressant Elavil my therapist had been prescribing for me, but I did not tell Zach this. It was my impression from certain remarks exchanged that the whiskey he and Mother were drinking was his, a gift bottle delivered upon another occasion. And that the pink limestone house of many rooms was his property. Before Zach left at 6 P.M. he used a downstairs bathroom, stomped down into the cellar to check out the furnace, made a telephone call in another room. Mother and I saw him to the door and saying good-bye to me he squeezed both my hands in his, murmuring *Ingrid!—good, good!* regarding me with approval, tenderness. He was not much taller than I was, but so solid, strong. He said *Good night, Chloe*, quickly, uncertainly as if his usual way of saying good night to her was not appropriate, in my presence. Mother shut the door after him and we watched him walk away through the swirling snow to his pickup truck, and at the truck he turned and waved, and Mother waved back.

In love with Chloe McDiarmid, but Chloe McDiarmid wasn't in love with him. So she was happy.

Telling me afterward what a wonderful man Zach Houston was, how good he'd been to her, kind, generous, thoughtful, a true gentleman. Protective of her but not possessive. Helped her through a hard time a few years ago, no need to go into details Mother said quietly. Lighting a cigarette Mother said, happily, "He likes you, honey. I could tell." I told Mother that I liked Zach, he seemed like a very nice man. "He is nice," Mother said, in that way of hers always mildly combative, "—but no fool." If I was wondering, Mother added, no Zach was *not* married, exactly; or, if he was, he'd been separated from his wife for a long, long time—"It's one of those pathetic cases, a woman hanging on to a man who doesn't love her, for pride's sake." But Mother didn't seem much disturbed. Going on to speak warmly of other friends in Mt. Ephraim, a few men, and women, two or three women like herself who'd been married and gone through hard times, children grown and gone, women friends she could talk and laugh with, go swimming at the Y with, share certain problems, feelings. "But nobody gets too close to me anymore," Mother said cheerfully, pouring an inch more whiskey into her glass. "I'd advise the same, honey, for you."

We were getting along well, I thought. The visit was going well. I would be staying overnight, driving back to Chautauqua Falls sometime the next day which was December 11, my birthday.

Strange how birthdays are celebrated, but not days of conception. For those are the days, the unknown days, hours, moments your fate begins.

Preparing a meal together in the big, old-fashioned kitchen. Cupboards to the ceiling, most of the shelves empty. A deep, stained sink equipped with a shiny new garbage disposal. A gas stove, gas oven, but a microwave oven on one of the counters, which

Mother said she didn't much like, didn't trust. She was brisk, whistling and humming. Giving directions always calling me *honey, sweetie*—the color up in her face from Zach's visit, the evidence of Zach's devotion, the good malt whiskey. When I'd been a girl in Mother's household there were certain mealtime tasks assigned to me and some of these I did now without needing to be told—scraping carrots, cutting the knotty eyes out of potatoes. Cleaning a heavy iron frying pan after Mother had used it to braise chicken pieces, wiping out the grease with a paper towel. A satisfaction in such simple tasks. And knowing too that I was making my mother happy,

You can make yourself well the doctor had told me. *It isn't me who will make you well, and it isn't any drug. Only you.*

Every drop of poison squeezed from my blood, my vow when I saw *You have to live: no choice* I would never take any drugs again would never give myself unquestioning to any man again, I saw things, people and objects both with a strange clarity. Like light radiated outward from them. Their weight, substance. If I touched, texture. I saw that these objects inhabited space and wasn't that proof that I too inhabited space, I *existed*, I *exist* and *I am.* Wasn't Ingrid Boone alive too, wasn't Ingrid Boone *here?* It did not seem to matter what was *inanimate, animate*—there was consciousness in everything. An old acid vision of mine that had gone wild, weird and scared the hell out of me but now in this calmness this clarity of being I saw that it was so. I touched objects with respect. I rarely touched people. I stared hard. There was always so much to learn. My sweet half smile that was a twitch of

my lips to greet people, queries, in the college class-
rooms in which I sat like any other student, though
more attentive, more diligent than most. My eyes that
were direct, level, sincere. My quietness, my courtesy.
My self-conscious good posture. My air of listening, and
of hearing. For all *here* is measured against *there*, a
dungeon stinking of garbage and feces. My weight was
nearly normal for my age, height, body build. My hair
had grown in so strangely thick and healthy, though
no longer curly, just a vague meandering wave. In
the hospital I'd met a woman not much older than I
who'd had breast cancer and chemotherapy and her
hair had fallen out entirely, straight hair that had
grown back in curly, tight-frizzy like the worst kind
of perm.

For all *here* is measured against *there*. Forever.

If I could not sleep through any night preferring to
sleep when I could during the day, or early evening, I
was sometimes able to sleep for as long as three hours
at a time before being wakened by quick flashes of
dreams, sweaty and shaking. I did not know if I was
sane, or what *sane* was. But I behaved as others did,
and that seemed to be all that was required. I could
tell by Mother's looks, words, frequent smiles, that she
was happy with me, relieved. There had been bad
times between us for many years, especially there had
been deceptions on my part, but these were past now.
I knew this, and Mother was coming to know it,
coming to trust me again.

She said suddenly, now the casserole was in the
oven, her voice low, thrilled, "Ingrid—I have some
things of your father's, and some things that remind
me of him. Want to see them?" Led me by the hand

into her bedroom at the rear of the house, switched on lights and I stood staring, in silence staring at the things displayed on windowsills, a bureau, a table. The blood-stiffened towel, the T-shirt, necktie. Laminated snapshots and glossy magazine photographs tacked to walls, maps of Florida and the Caribbean. A man's russet-brown hat, a man's gold wristwatch. A single playing card—the joker. Certain of these items I recognized and others I did not. My mind was rushing, my thoughts flew too fast to be comprehended. There was a roaring in my ears. Mother watched my face, she'd lit a cigarette and the smoke stung my eyes. I wiped at my eyes. Mother was moving excitedly about, touching things, adjusting them, brushing at dust, a strand of cobweb. She spoke rapidly laughing in that high breathless way she'd laughed over the telephone as if to discount the gravity of her words even as they were uttered. I stood in silence blinking and staring at these things, the evidence of Mother's love, Mother's madness, not knowing what to say. She told me I was the first person, I would be the only person ever to be allowed in here. She told me it not because I was her daughter but I was his daughter, and he'd loved me so. He'd loved her, and he'd loved me. So much. Not like any ordinary man. So much. With shaky fingers Mother was striking matches, one by one she lit a row of incense candles, squat little candles like the votary candles in Roman Catholic churches, to illuminate the Kodak snapshots. The cloying-sweet incense smell made me feel slightly sick. Mother was saying, almost angry, belligerent, "No one else can know. Just you and me. Nobody else's Goddamned business, right?"

We stood for a while in the bedroom, contemplating

the display. Outside the wind was blowing, gritty snow-flakes, bits of sleet thrown against the windows. The room was drafty, the bed thick-piled with a blanket and a handmade quilt. So Zach Houston had never entered this room, and would never. Why this struck me as sad, I don't know.

I said, the effort like dredging up words buried in mud, "The way it has to be is to know you exist even when you're not in pain. . . ." My voice trailed off, maybe I hadn't spoken aloud.

Mother was relighting one of the little candles and seemed not to have heard. Sometimes it happens even now, every drop of poison squeezed from my blood, I believe I have spoken aloud but I have not.

Or I have heard a voice, and I have not.

Mother said carefully, "If you want anything here, Ingrid, please take it. It would make me so happy if you would."

I tried to tell Mother I didn't want any of her things. Thank you Mother I said but I didn't want any of her things. I was frightened of her things, I did not even want to touch them, or look too closely. But again Mother seemed not to hear. She was smoking her ciga-rette in that old way of quick short panting puffs, she was moving about the room smiling, excited and anx-ious and glancing at me sidelong as if in dread of seeing in my face what I would not allow to be seen. "It would make me so happy," she said, "—just to know they were in two places, you know?—so, if there was a fire or something in one, the other would be safe. You know?"

I picked out one of the laminated snapshots, one I recognized from my father's last visit, taken at the

Marsena airport of Lucas Boone, Chloe Boone, Ingrid as a little girl kicking in the air, and I picked out the joker because it was an easy choice, so small and impersonal and I could throw it away with no regret, and because Mother was waiting, silently urging me to take something more I picked out a crumpled pack of Camels reasoning that Mother could so easily replace it. Other items were a man's black plastic pocket comb, dirty, some of its teeth missing, and a key chain with a carved wooden dog's head. There was a fancy silver ballpoint pen that could never have been a pen of my father's. There was a fake-gold cigarette lighter scrolled with the initials JKV. Atop the bureau was a tall green vase, its fluted rim partly broken, a beautiful vase into which Mother had stuck dried cattails and marsh grass and hawks' wing feathers.

Quietly Mother had come up behind me, embraced me now nudging her head against mine and leaning against me, her warm fleshy weight, her need. I stiffened in terror that she would cry, and so I would cry, and would not be able to stop. But her voice was vaguely scornful, she gestured with her hand holding the cigarette toward the window, the vast world beyond the window—"They say he's dead, the fuckers, but I don't believe it, do you?"

Brought our meal on trays into the sewing room, the kitchen table was too heaped with clutter and anyway, Mother said, this was her favorite room. She'd brought the poinsettia plant in too, set it on the ironing board by a window where we could admire it as we ate. Never seen such a beautiful poinsettia, Mother insisted.

Mother's sewing room was high-ceilinged and drafty like the other rooms I'd seen, but the windows had bright chintz curtains and the space was cozy, comfortably cluttered with Mother's sewing things. There were bolts of colorful cloth, *Vogue*, Butterick, Simplicity dress patterns, a new-looking Singer sewing machine, trim, ribbons, dressmaker's scissors, boxes of thread of all colors, a giant pumpkin-pincushion glinting with pins and needles. There were two dressmaker's dummies, one fairly slender and the other matronly with ample hips, breasts. The matronly one was fitted with an electric-blue satin dress, a mother-of-the-bride's dress Mother identified it, naming a name I recognized, the family name of a Mt. Ephraim businessman. Most of the equipment had belonged to Flora Wells, Mother said. She'd left Mother lots of items from the shop, though no money. "I didn't really expect anything," Mother said quickly. "Though I was the poor woman's closest friend, the last year of her life. I did the books for her, I put in extra hours at the shop, visited with her all the time in the hospital, and at home. People stopped coming. Even relatives. Poor Flora had been such a bitch, you know—*you* remember—a real tyrant, 'career woman'—but we got along, she liked me, no bullshitting *me* and I knew not to bullshit her. Jesus, she weighed only about sixty pounds at the end. Cancer—ugh! But any way you die so slow, old Mr. Houston, Zach's father, he's ninety and had a stroke a few years ago and—well, you know. Zach says better to go quick as you can, when you can." Mother paused, avoiding my eyes as I was avoiding hers. Adding then, in a softer voice, "Anyway, I'd sit with the old girl. She hated TV so I'd sit with

her, do some sewing and Flora would talk, talk. I tried
to listen, because the poor woman was so alone.
Here's a woman never married, never had any kids—
never been in love she'd boasted, can you believe it?—
yet she's got so much to talk about, Jesus she'd had a
life. So I tried to listen, but you know how you drift
into your own thoughts. I always have my own
thoughts. When I was with your father of course I
didn't, I'd be just with him but now I have my own
thoughts I can draw upon. I have my own good
memories."

Mother was sipping whiskey while she ate, small
sips between forkfuls of the chicken casserole. I drank
just water, from the kitchen tap. The food was delicious and I was very hungry but ate slowly as I need to
eat, not talking much. Each mouthful chewed and pre-
meditated, swallowed with caution lest my stomach
will reject it for once my stomach had been so
shrunken I'd screamed in the agony of eating, writhed
like a worm on a fisherman's hook. But now I was all
right. If I was careful. It was just the thought sometimes of certain visions, memories, tastes in my
mouth, the stench of rotting garbage intervening
between my appetite and what was on my fork lifted
to my mouth like a shadow slicing the air. But it was
only a shadow, it was *not-here*. It was nothing.

We were sitting side by side on a handsome sofa
now slightly shabby, each arm torn as if by cats' claws.
We were eating from large white dinner plates with a
delicate floral pattern and with silver-plate cutlery I'd
never seen before. The dummy wearing the electric-
blue dress was to the left, at the periphery of my vision
so it seemed there was a third party present, mute but

observing. The other dummy, naked, stood in a rear corner. As we ate, and Mother chattered, we kept glancing up at the window before us where, by day, the river would probably have been visible, but now it was dark, just past 8 P.M. and black as midnight. And the wind with its human-sounding wail, you never really get used to—I'd been hearing it back in Chautauqua Falls, in my own bedroom, in my own bed. Whether I was with another person in that bed, or alone. And the snowstorm—spirals and waterfalls of snow, driving sleet, illuminated in the light spilling out from the window. What a strange new place this is, I thought. I was happy suddenly. I was hungry, and I was happy. I've never been here before, I thought. But this could be my home.

Mother set aside her plate, jumped to her feet as if she'd just now remembered. Her birthday present for me—a long-sleeved blouse she'd sewed, white raw silk. "Here, honey. I almost forgot. For you." I stood, and held it against myself. It was a beautiful blouse, the buttons mother-of-pearl, the hand-stitching exquisite. It looked as if it might be a little too large for me but I thanked Mother, I told her it was beautiful, the most beautiful blouse I'd ever owned, or seen. She was looking at me almost shyly. "You can try it on, later. I can take it in, you know. The bust. It's about thirty-four, that's maybe too big."

I came to Mother and kissed her, somewhat clumsily hugging her, my arms thin, weak. Mother laughed and hugged *me*. She'd kicked off her shoes, standing now in her stockinged feet, so much shorter than I'd have believed.

We sat down again. Mother lit another cigarette.

Didn't offer me one, but tossed the pack down where I could reach it if I wanted. She exhaled smoke in a long sigh, crossed her legs in a mannish gesture. "Y'know, I quit smoking last year—visiting Flora, I got out of the habit. Can't remember when I started again."

I said, these words dredged up from someone I'd overheard, or a conversation I'd had, "Once you start smoking again, it's like you've never quit."

"*You've* quit?"

"No. I'm just not smoking."

Mother spoke of Zach Houston for a while, what a good man he was, he dropped by for supper three or four evenings a week, they got along well, had she told me how he'd helped her pull through a bad time a few years ago?—and no questions asked, or not many. "There aren't many men like that," Mother said. She laughed, and shook ashes into a big glass ashtray. Looking at me sidelong, a shy smile. "What is your life now, honey? You're taking courses at the college, and you're working in an office, and I have an address for you, where you're living, and—what else?"

I said, "I'm thinking of getting married. In the spring."

Mother said evenly, "Who is he?"

Suddenly I was shy, telling her of you.

What I knew of you.

That you'd been my therapist at the clinic; that you were fourteen years older than me, and divorced. That you seemed to love me very much. That you weren't my doctor any longer; we hadn't been seeing each other in that way until after the therapy was finished. That you said you'd loved me for a long time. You'd said, *I'm a doctor, I don't judge.*

Mother listened. Mother smoked her cigarette and did not inquire if I was in love. From the tone of my voice, my calm measured voice, she knew.

She said so softly I almost couldn't hear, "Well. Will I meet him sometime, this 'doctor' of yours?" Her eyes shone with tears. She wiped them, quickly. Leaning over then to kiss me and losing her balance so she fell against me and suddenly the two of us were laughing together breathless as girls. Mother was a little drunk, I realized. And it seemed that I was a little drunk, too, though I'd had only ice water. We laughed, our laughter hurt. We rose then self-consciously and carried our trays back into the kitchen and rinsed our plates in the sink and with a flourish Mother opened a cupboard door and there was a double-layer cake— "Angel food, sweetie, your favorite, remember?" She'd baked it herself from a Pillsbury mix, vanilla meringue frosting. Pink sugar letters spelled out HAPPY BIRTH-DAY INGRID and there were twenty-one pink candles on the cake, some of them crooked, fallen. We laughed straightening them and in the sewing room Mother lit them carefully one by one, steadying her right hand by holding the wrist with her left hand, frowning with the effort. "Blow out the candles, honey. Make a wish." I made a silent wish *I wish to do the right thing always, to love the right people* and blew out the candles awkwardly, missing some so Mother joined in to help.

Mother said, squeezing my hand, "I made a wish, too. O.K.?"

We returned to the sofa to eat our cake, but I became sleepy suddenly, I could hardly lift my fork though it was delicious. I told Mother, "I've never tasted cake so . . . delicious." But the words were vague like dream words. I could not keep my eyes open. I wasn't sure if I'd spoken. The wind and the swirling snow and my warm coursing blood had hypnotized me. At about the distance of the river was the muffled cry *Dog-girl! Dog-girl!* which I did not hear for Mother was smoking another cigarette and complaining she wished she hadn't started smoking again, I was Goddamned smart to quit, maybe she'd quit again, too. My eyelids were so heavy, my senses dulled, I could barely hear Mother's voice. She yawned, she stretched, sighed. Said, "Sometimes I think, I'm so happy here. How can I deserve to be so happy?"

EPILOGUE:

The First Morning of Creation

There's the morning you're wakened by wind and light and when you look outside, everything is ice. A frieze of ice. Storm damage everywhere, tree limbs and entire trees collapsed beneath the weight of ice shining with such a glare you can hardly see. The river, too, laced with ice at the shores notched like teeth but at its center free-running, dark rushing artery of something too dense and sinewy to be only water.

Mother says *O Jesus it's like the first morning of creation, a morning like this. You know why you're alive,* Mother says, laughing rubbing her eyes. *Even with a hangover.*

Went outside in a borrowed jacket, boots, a man's wool cap I found hanging on a hook in the kitchen, to inspect my borrowed Camaro, coated in ice. Windshield coated like a washboard, even the door handles iced over. I walked stumbling through the crusted snow staring, dazzled blind by ice, so many glittering points of ice. This strange beautiful new place, I thought. What is it?

Almost, I felt scared.

I saw the sun on fire at the ridge of tall juniper firs to the rear of the stone house. And smoke lifting from the chimney of that house. Frost in the air so my nostrils flamed.

Ingrid! Ingrid! Ingrid! You're still alive.

I heard that voice, I thought it must be yours. For I did love you—I love you. Of that, I have certain knowledge.

I was walking outside for a long time it seemed. My breath steaming and my eyes watering at first, then getting used to the cold. Just at zero Fahrenheit the radio news would say. And a wind driving it colder. But I'm used to cold. When I looked more closely I saw that much of the storm damage wasn't new. Old mounds of debris beside the road, fallen and broken fir trees behind the house that must have been there for a long time, maybe a year. Years. Tall desiccated weeds were poking through them, suckers and scrawny little trees. You wondered how they could survive but of course they did. In the skin were marks just visible through the ice-coating, like a secret writing, scars. Nor were they dead exactly, those fallen trees. They were alive, only not vertical. The heartbeat inside them had maybe slowed, only a murmur but if you squatted to listen, if you knew how to listen, if the wind would die down you would hear it.